Jack raced over the hill's flat summit toward a stand of hardwoods, and stood quietly by a tree. It was an orthodox move; a fox, running where Thunder's voice said it was, should come to the hardwoods. Thunder's baying strengthened, and Jack tensed himself. He had guessed correctly; the Haunt Fox was coming. A moment later Jack saw him and brought the shotgun to his shoulder . . .

Haunt Fox

"Exceptionally good nature writing in a fast-moving story of a red fox whose ability to evade traps, hounds and hunters earned him the name of Haunt Fox, and of the boy and hound who hunted him."

—Booklist

"Boy, dog and fox are sharply drawn and endowed with life and individuality."

—The New York Times

"One of Mr. Kjelgaard's best books"

—Horn Book

Bantam Books by Jim Kjelgaard
Ask your bookseller for the books you have missed

Haunt Fox

Jim Kjelgaard

Drawings by Glen Rounds

BANTAM BOOKS
TORONTO · NEW YORK · LONDON · SYDNEY · AUCKLAND

*This low-priced Bantam Book
has been completely reset in a type face
designed for easy reading, and was printed
from new plates. It contains the complete
text of the original hard-cover edition.*
NOT ONE WORD HAS BEEN OMITTED.

RL 6, 010-014

HAUNT FOX
*A Bantam Book / published by arrangement with
Holiday House Inc.*

PRINTING HISTORY
*Holiday House edition published 1954
Bantam edition / September 1981
2nd printing . . . April 1985*

ISBN 0-553-15368-4

Published simultaneously in the United States and Canada

---

*Bantam Books are published by Bantam Books, Inc. Its trade-
mark, consisting of the words "Bantam Books" and the por-
trayal of a rooster, is Registered in U.S. Patent and Trademark
Office and in other countries. Marca Registrada. Bantam
Books, Inc., 666 Fifth Avenue, New York, New York 10103.*

PRINTED IN THE UNITED STATES OF AMERICA

CW   11 10 9 8 7 6 5 4 3 2

For Irvin Kerlan

Contents

Chapter 1   The Raider

It was a night so dark that only the unwise, the very young, or the desperately hungry ventured far from the thickets, swamps, and burrows where wild things find shelter in times of stress.

The sky was full of murky clouds that surged and rolled like the waves of some fantastic black sea. A brisk wind blew through the leafless maples, birches, and aspens, and rattled the shriveled leaves that still clung to the gnarled oaks and the smaller beeches. Copses of hemlock and stands of pine bent their heads in the darkness and seemed to whisper among themselves.

Through this moonless, starless, dangerous night

traveled two young foxes. They were Star and his blood brother, Brush.

They were among the very young, for only one spring and summer had passed since their birth in a hillside den. The summer had been a good and joyous time, a time of play and growth. Star and Brush, much like any young puppies anywhere, had scuffled and wrestled with each other and with their three sisters. Later they had followed their mother and father away from the den and had, after a fashion, learned to hunt. They knew a great deal about mice and rabbits. They had been taught something about low branches where night-roosting birds might be found, and they knew a little of the splay-footed snowshoe hares that were so fast and hard to catch. Star and Brush knew just enough to take care of themselves and, providing a good deal of luck remained on their side, to survive in the wilderness.

From the day they had been born, they had been together. Always, when all five cubs had a free-for-all scramble, it had ended up with Star and Brush, side by side, defending a rock, a bit of grass, or a tiny hemlock at one side of their den. They had hunted together when they first followed their father and mother on hunts and they had never strayed apart since.

They didn't know where their mother and three sisters were and that was as well for them, because the stretched pelts of all four hung on drying boards in Dade Matson's fur room. Fox pelts were not yet prime, but there was a two-dollar bounty on every fox caught and it was said in the hills that Dade Matson would do anything for money except work.

The father of the brood, a big, dark-colored, handsome dog fox of extreme wisdom and cunning, knew all about what had happened to his mate and daughters. Now he had gone off by himself to become a wandering, surly, lonesome creature. Already old, as a fox's age is reckoned, he would never take another mate. And he wanted nothing more to do with his sons, for within the dog fox lived an ancient fear. For years he had reigned supreme among his kind. But it is an unchangeable law that, no matter how mighty one individual may become, he cannot rule forever because the young will take the place of the old. Therefore the old dog fox hated and feared his sons and chased them every time their paths crossed. The only reason he never caught and killed them was because they could run faster than he.

Star and Brush were abroad because they were hungry. Had they been older and wiser they would have borne the pangs of hunger, as their father was doing, and stayed near some thicket or burrow where they could find shelter in a hurry. But nothing in the experience of either had taught them that yet.

Star walked a little ahead of his brother as they skirted a laurel thicket where they hoped to find an unwary rabbit. Already almost as big as his father, needing only time to achieve full adult strength and sturdiness, Star had fur much darker than that of the average red fox. His brush, or tail, was so long and so well-furred that it seemed to be a graceful extension of his body. His black-tipped ears were pointed, like those of a police dog, and within his eyes glowed a great intelligence that would one day be wisdom. Squarely in the center of his chest was a star-shaped white spot.

Brush, his brother, was slightly smaller, lighter-coated, and not as strong. Nor did he have that indefinable quality that marked Star as a born leader of his kind.

Star halted in his tracks and used his pointed nose to sift the air currents that swirled about him. He had caught the faint odor of roosting grouse. Just behind him, Brush stopped too. Brush waited for Star to make the first definite move, but for the space of perhaps two minutes Star did not move at all.

They were near a little swamp wherein grew aspens, hemlocks, birches, laurel and rho-dodendron, and a few pine trees. Star knew that the grouse were in the swamp, but he could not deter-mine exactly where they were. He remained poised, all four feet resting lightly, as he strove to analyze the wind currents.

Mingled with the scent of the grouse was that of a doe deer who was also feeding in the swamp. There was a stale odor of rabbits that had played some hours past, the smell of a skunk that had been abroad lately but was now sleeping under a hollow stump, and the fetid odor of a hibernating bear. Star sifted all the smells carefully.

He was not interested in the doe; she was too big to be pulled down by foxes. The skunk, he knew from sad past experience, was better let alone, and the bear held no promise of anything. But the grouse did.

Star tilted his nose, sifting the various wind currents. He caught the grouse scent firmly and began to follow it. But he did not know how to keep it in his nose, and a second later the odor was again lost. Star stopped short. He swung around to touch noses with his brother.

When Star started out again he went in a straight line, still keeping the wind in his nose. Though he was not an expert hunter, he knew enough about grouse to know that they would be roosting, on a night like this, in some shelter where the wind could not strike them directly.

He was right. They were in a thicket of hemlocks, where little trees grew so closely together, and were so thickly plastered with needles, that not even the roughest wind could reach the center. With Brush his silent shadow, Star slipped into the thicket and threaded his way among the small trees. The scent was strong enough now so that there was no mistaking it.

But Star had his first feeling of failure long before he reached the tree in which the grouse roosted. The steady current carrying the grouse's scent came from high up. Therefore, the birds must be out of reach.

Star came to the tallest hemlock in the thicket and verified what he already suspected. Low enough so that surrounding trees broke the force of the wind, but high enough so that no ground-prowler could possibly reach them, the five roosting grouse were comfortably asleep on a branch.

In spite of their disappointment, the two young foxes made no noise. If the grouse thought themselves safe, they would continue to roost in the hemlocks. Some other night, they might choose the lower branches and thus put themselves within striking range.

Star paused once more to sniff noses with his brother, then hesitated uncertainly. The wind was driving very hard. A few snowflakes whisked along on it and pattered crisply against frozen foliage. Star had an uneasy foreboding, but did not know, as more experienced creatures would, that a mighty storm was in the making.

Ahead of them the leaves rustled, and Star leaped high to come down on the moving leaves with both fore paws. It was an approved way of catching mice, but Star had yet to perfect the technique. The mouse that had rustled the leaves slipped between his paws and dived into a subterranean burrow. Star sniffled at the warm scent and licked hungry chops.

Brush edged impatiently past, and Star made no move to take the lead again. Turning from the line of march Star had set, Brush slid under a rusting wire fence and started uphill toward a patch of laurel. Star followed willingly. The hilltop was the home of numerous snowshoe hares and, though they had yet to catch one, there was always the hope that somehow they might. The snowshoes, who almost never sought protection, would be abroad even on a night like this.

Trotting so smoothly that they almost seemed to flow along, Star and Brush reached the top of the hill and entered the laurel thicket. For a few minutes, because so doing enabled him to take an easier route, Brush led them with the wind instead of against it. Star nervously flicked his alert ears and slowed his pace a little. They passed beneath a wind-felled tree with a crooked trunk.

Disaster struck so suddenly that it appeared, was

upon them, and had overwhelmed Brush, before Star fully knew what was happening. Then he did know, and all in a split second he leaped away. Tail curled tightly against his haunches, his eyes wrinkled as his face formed a savage snarl.

Facing him, and no more than a yard away, was Stub, the wild cat. An old and evil pirate of the hills, for the past two weeks Stub had made his lair in the heart of the laurel thicket and lived on the snowshoes. He was a cunning hunter, a creature that was never seen until he struck, and then he killed so swiftly that his victims seldom had anything except a fleeting glimpse of him. Tonight Stub had been crouching on the fallen tree, waiting for a snowshoe, but a young fox was even more acceptable.

He stood with both front paws on the inert form of Brush, growling under his breath and looking with his yellow cat's eyes at Star. He was not afraid. Stub, who could attack and kill a full-grown deer, feared nothing except Dade Matson.

There was born in Star a sudden chill that had nothing to do with the wind or the cold night. At the same instant, though he gave ground, he felt an anger rising to hatred for this thing that struck so silently and so lethally. Yet he dared not fight.

Star whirled suddenly and fled. He felt intense hatred, but at the same time he could not conquer fear. Stub had come from nowhere to strike and kill.

Star's eyes were desperate, his jaws widespread, as he ran from the awful creature that had murdered his brother.

He did not halt until he had run clear out of the thicket and stood again at the foot of the hill. There, for a moment, he trembled. Then he gazed back toward the thicket, where Brush lay dead under Stub's taloned paws. Twice Star snapped his jaws, and the sound was like that of a snapping steel trap. Firmly in his brain he fixed the scent and physical aspects of Stub; he would know him when they met again.

The wind was waning, but now huge snowflakes drifted like oversized feathers out of the churning cloud banks. They fell so fast that, almost within a matter of minutes, the frozen ground became white and the frost-shriveled grass was hidden. This was to be the Great Snow, the most terrible storm in the memory of the oldest inhabitant. It would spill out of the sky until morning came again, continue to fall throughout the day, and while another moonless night blackened the wilderness. The first flowers of April would bloom again before the wild things could consider themselves safe, and the melting snow would reveal many a skeleton forlorn in wet leaves.

Now, Star knew only that the snow was unfamiliar stuff that made his paws cold. One by one he lifted them, held them for a few seconds against his heavy fur, and put them back down in the snow. Bewildered and uncertain, he stood still.

So far the night's hunt had brought only tragedy. But tragedy was something all wild things had to accept. They existed by violence and, almost without exception, all of them died violently. However, no matter what happened or who died, the living must still fill their bellies, and Star was very hungry.

He was also at a loss. Already, with Brush, he had visited the places where they had always found food, but had discovered nothing. The snowshoe thicket remained, but snowshoes were hard to catch under any circumstances and Stub patrolled the thicket. Star knew that he dared not risk a fang to fang battle with the big cat.

He slithered through a barbed-wire fence without touching the wire and trotted through the deepening snow toward the last place he knew. It was the farm of Jeff Crowley. Nestled in a valley between two gently sloping hills, the farm consisted of broad fields and pastures, a snug house, a comfortable barn, a poultry house, a pigpen, an icehouse, and various smaller outbuildings. But that was only its outward aspect. In addition, the farm had a thousand fascinations for a young fox.

More than once, lying concealed in some thicket, Star had watched, entranced, while Jeff Crowley's cows grazed in their summer-green pastures. Star had gone forward to sniff long and searchingly of their tracks after the cows were driven home to be milked, and, as he came to know them, he had even shown himself to them. They had only stared, mildly astonished at such a thing as a fox. Though they were huge and powerful creatures, they were not at all belligerent. Star had satisfied himself that there was no harm in the cows.

Many times, remaining hidden himself, Star had also gazed in entranced wonder as the men from the farm drove teams of horses about the fields. They plowed, or hauled crops, or cut hay, or did other unexplainable things which men and horses seemed always to be doing when they were together. But Star had never shown himself to the men; he had an inborn fear of human beings.

There was still much about the farm that Star had investigated only with his keen nose. These odors he had caught were far and away the most fascinating part of Crowley's farm.

There were the scents of chickens, geese, and ducks. Star knew the heavy odor of the pigs in their sty, and the tempting aroma of mice and rats in the barn and the granary. He had wrinkled his nose at the various, and to him unsavory, scents that drifted from the farmhouse. He knew the smell of wood smoke that came from the house's chimney and the acrid taint of coal smoke when coal was burned in the farm's forge. There was little about the farm that his nose had not told him, but he still did not know enough.

One of his traits, a very marked one, was a mighty curiosity about anything and everything. A leaf blowing in the wind, if he could not identify it from a distance, was enough to swerve him two hundred yards so that he might make a thorough investigation. Once, raptly intent, he had stood for a whole hour just watching the shadows in a sun-dappled pool. Again, he had lain beneath a tall tree for half a day because, high in the branches, a chickaree, or red squirrel, was occasionally flicking its tail.

So, as he investigated everything else, he longed to investigate the farm at close range and, possibly, find something to eat. But there had always been humans either present or close by and he was afraid of human scent. Even at night he had not dared go near this strange place which people inhabited. He padded uncertainly back and forth.

The snow fell very thickly, coming down so fast and in such huge flakes that Star blinked his eyes against them. Already the ground was covered almost halfway to his hocks, so that when he moved he left a furrow instead of a trail behind him. Again Star lifted his cold paws and warmed them against his thick fur.

After fifteen minutes he turned and trotted straight toward the barnyard. Into the wind he traveled, and when the wind shifted he changed his course to stay in it. As he advanced, he used his nose to keep him informed of what lay ahead.

Mingled with the stream of odors that came to him was one which he could not at once identify, and Star halted. It was, he knew, the odor of a dog. Many times Star had smelled the two shaggy farm dogs. But this was a new and unfamiliar beast. There was about it the fresh scent of a young creature not much older than Star himself, and there was nothing unduly menacing about the scent.

For the first time Star had smelled Thunder, fourteen-year-old Jack Crowley's gangling foxhound puppy. At the present time, sheltered from the wind and snow in a warm niche on the Crowleys' back porch, Thunder lay fast asleep, his paws twitching as he slept.

Star stalked into the barnyard. He snuffled around the barn where cattle contentedly chewed their cuds in warm stalls and draft horses shuffled their heavy feet. The stable's door was shut and locked, but enticing odors drifted through a slight crack which the door did not cover completely. Star drooled at the scents, for among them was that of mice which were scurrying back and forth to pick up bits of grain that the munching cattle and horses had knocked from their feeding bins.

Star went from the barn door to the pigpen, sniffed disinterestedly at four fat black and white pigs that never even stirred when he came near, then stiffened to attention.

Nearby was a squat shed with a closed back but an open front, and in it were stored a wagon, a hay rake, a plow, a disk harrow, and a light cart with a leather top. In back of these were some discarded boards and old machinery, including a broken cultivator. On the cross bar, four chickens had sought a night's roost. Ordinarily they would have been in the fox-proof poultry house with the rest of the chickens, but in the hurry to get things done before the storm that the Crowleys knew was approaching, nobody had had time to bother with four stray chickens.

Star stole into the shed and tilted his pointed nose, while a gleam lighted both eyes. Fat, stupid, domestic fowl, the chickens' eyes were closed and they were fast asleep. No danger had ever disturbed their lives and they expected none now. They were so close to the ground that Star had only to stalk forward, rear with one fore paw beside the chickens, open his mouth, and snap once. But in that second, something happened.

In the eye wink before death stilled it, the chicken Star grabbed uttered a strangled, piercing squawk. Not yet knowing what had happened, aware only that something was wrong, the other three hens began to cackle.

Star wasted no time. The heavy chicken weighed

almost half as much as he himself did, but Star snatched it by the neck, threw the body over his back, and sped into the night. He had scarcely cleared the shed when the night was split by another sound.

It was a rolling bass roar, a thunder that rose even above the screaming wind. Thunder, the foxhound, had heard the chickens and at once had come awake. A stray breeze brought him Star's scent and Thunder accepted the challenge. Thus the ancient chase was on once more; the foxhound was in pursuit of the fox.

The desperately laboring Star took a firmer grip on his pirated booty and ran as fast as he could. But even as he ran he knew that Thunder was closing the gap between them.

Chapter 2 Failure

For most of his fourteen years, Jack Crowley had heard about foxhounds and fox hunts. During his own youth, Jack's father had been a tireless hunter, and still thought that, of all hunting, the very finest was driving foxes with a good hound. So did Joe Mason, who owned the farm next to theirs, and Perry Albright, who drove the milk truck. During winter evenings the men had gathered at the Crowley farm and lived again, in memory, hunts of the past. It was true that none of them owned a hound now nor did they even go hunting except on an occasional afternoon. But they still liked to talk about it, and Jack never tired of listening.

16

Sometimes Dade Matson joined the group. He was always welcome, but there was something about Dade that Jack did not like. He was older than any of the others, and unlike them. They were warm and human, but he was cold. Where their eyes shone as they recalled some especially memorable hunt, or talked of bugle-voiced hounds on a trail, Dade's never did. He only recalled how much money he had received for special pelts.

Quiet by nature, Jack had always sat close to the men, missing no word they said. And during those winter evenings, while the wind howled outside and frost glittered on the windows, his dream had been born. He must have a foxhound himself. He had to know the fun that these quiet, competent men had known. For when they discussed foxhounds and fox hunting they were excited as they were at no other time.

So the summer before, when his farm chores were done, Jack had pedaled his bicycle three miles to the village of Carneyville to pick up a bundle of papers and deliver them to the various farmhouses along the road. He had saved every penny, and in August he bought Thunder.

Jack had chosen him himself from among five hound puppies, all the same age and outwardly as alike as leaves on a maple. But in other ways they were as different as Jack's father and Dade Matson.

Four of the puppies had wagged up and reared

against the fence that enclosed them, begging for attention. Though willing to be friendly, even at the age of four and a half months Thunder had not been one to fling himself at any casual stranger. However, when Jack had opened the gate and gone in, Thunder did not run away. Gravely he sniffed Jack over, and experimentally licked Jack's hand. With a leash on his neck, he had trotted willingly along when Jack paid for him.

Then, in Jack's mind, had arisen a little cloud of worry. He had earned the money to pay for Thunder and he had chosen him. But what would his father say now? Not about having the dog, for from the first his father and mother had agreed that he might have it. What would he say *about* the dog?

He had taken Thunder home, and as soon as he arrived his father came to see the puppy. He was a big, sad-eyed hound with a black upper body, tan lower, and a thin tail. His long ears, black on the outer side and tan on the inner, came within a few inches of the ground as he walked, and he wore a perpetually mournful expression. But within his sad eyes were both gentleness and a deep intelligence. Heavy jowls sagged across his jaws, but his jowls were the only flabby part of Thunder. His legs were long and strong, his chest massive, and his body well-proportioned. His black nose seemed eternally to be questing for some scent. He was a trailing hound of the best type, and his ancestry extended back so far that the beginnings were lost in the mist of time.

There was an overlong inspection as Jeff's father looked at Thunder's chest, his ears, his padded paws, his tail, and even opened his mouth to look inside that. Then his father had rendered the all-important verdict.

"Well, he may be a hound some day."

It was more than enough; coming from his father, it was the highest praise. Thunder became a member of the farm family though, as Jeff pointed out, he was not a house dog. Let him live with the wind, the weather, and the worst and best the elements might offer. A hunting hound had to know and to meet all of it. So Jack had fixed him a bed on the porch, between the woodbox and the wall.

The night Star stole the chicken, Jack was fast asleep when Thunder bayed. Even then, Jack was not sure that he awakened at all; he seemed to be living in a dream, a dream that echoed with the musical thunder of a bell-mouthed foxhound. Jack stirred in his bed, vaguely aware that he should get up and find out about it. Then he went back to sleep.

The next time he awakened, a very dim light filtered through the curtains in his room. Jack yawned and stretched, and came completely awake. He sprang out of bed, shivered as his bare feet struck the cold floor, and padded over to look out the window. A gasp of delight escaped him when he saw the thickly driving snow. His father had always said that hounds run best on good snow.

Jack wriggled into his clothes and ran down into the kitchen, where the big woodstove cast a welcome heat. The big clock that ticked steadily away on the wall said a quarter to seven and only a faint forerunner of daylight slanted against the windows. Jack thought of the still-falling snow, and of the many tasks it was sure to bring. There would be drifts to break away so doors could be opened, paths and roads to clear, the woodpile to uncover, and all the dozen things that they had probably forgotten to do yesterday afternoon. Then, somehow, the chores would have to be worked in.

Jack warmed his shoes beside the stove and sat down in a corner, near the woodbox, to put them on. His mother was already cooking breakfast. She finished mixing batter in a bowl and began to drop pancakes onto a steaming griddle where round patties of sausage were already browning. Jack licked his lips.

Today, certainly, the school buses would be unable to get through the snow. He and his father would work around the farm and do whatever needed doing. Tomorrow, Jack hoped, the roads would still be blocked and the farm work caught up. He looked again out of the nearly dark window, toward the hills. Tomorrow there was some hope of getting out with Thunder.

It was true that Thunder was only an eight-month-old puppy and his father had said that it was not wise to expect too much out of him this winter. He might trail a little but probably wouldn't yet be old enough to understand what trailing was all about. Still, all dogs had to start sometime.

Jack continued to stare out of the window, and only his body remained in the kitchen. The rest of him, the part that mattered, was out in the hills. Thunder was tonguing strongly on a hot trail and his rolling roars echoed back. Jack raised his shotgun, drew down on a running fox, and—

"Jack!"

Jack looked guiltily up to see that his mother had put the wheat cakes and sausage in separate dishes on the table. His father was sitting down to eat, a faint smile on his face. A big man, who could fight a fractious horse to a standstill or toss a hundred-pound bag of grain on a wagon, Jeff Crowley was still very gentle and understanding.

"Better come and eat, Bub," his father said.

Jack wrenched himself away from the hills and Thunder. Back in the kitchen, he realized with a start how hungry he was. It did seem that he was always hungry, not only at meal times but whenever he thought about eating.

Jeff forked six pancakes and three sausage patties on his plate and Jack took the same. He lathered the pancakes with fresh butter and drowned the whole plateful in maple syrup. Then he began to shovel it into his mouth.

"Don't eat so fast," his mother admonished.

"Sorry, Ma," Jack mumbled.

He dropped his fork and stared vacantly across the table. Again, in his mind, he was up in the hills with Thunder. He would not, he felt, even need a shotgun if Thunder really knew how to trail a fox.

"I declare!" his mother said. "That boy either eats like a pig or he doesn't eat at all!"

His father said, "Would you be thinking of the fresh snow, and a fox hunt?"

"That's right!" Jack said. His father always seemed to know.

"Forget it," Jeff advised. "You'll have to wait for a crust anyhow; no hound could run in this. Besides, there's work to be done. Have some more pancakes."

Jack took three more pancakes and one more sausage patty. Then he ate a piece of apple pie and suddenly wasn't hungry any more. He looked at the big stack of pancakes and the four patties that were left. Thunder would have a hearty breakfast, too.

"I'll feed Thunder," he said.

His father reached for the coffeepot. "Do that.

Then we'd better get started. It's quarter past seven already."

Jack buckled on knee-length rubber overshoes so that they came outside his trousers. He put on a wool jacket, and a cap with a strap that buckled beneath his chin. He thrust wool mittens into his pocket, picked up the plate of pancakes and sausage, and went out to find Thunder's dish.

Thunder always knew when he might expect breakfast and was always at the back door to greet Jack with wagging tail and a hand-licking tongue. But this morning he was not there, and for a long while he had not been there. The space between the woodbox and the wall, where Thunder usually slept, was drifted over with snowflakes. Had Thunder been there or even if he had slept there lately, his body heat would have melted the snow.

Jack stared hopelessly into the snow draperies that hid the barn and almost blotted out the lilacs, thirty feet from the porch. Last night's dream, the voice of a foxhound cutting through the storm, came again to him. In that dismal moment he knew that he wouldn't find Thunder at the barn or in any of the sheds. On the trail of a fox, his beloved hound was somewhere out in the storm. Jack felt a sickness in the pit of his stomach.

The hand that held the breakfast he had intended to give Thunder was limp as he went back into the house. He put the plate on the table and stared at it unseeingly. His father's voice broke the wall of misery that engulfed him.

"What's the matter, Bub?"

"Thunder's gone."

"I expect he went to the barn, or the shed."

"No, he didn't."

"How do you know he didn't?"

"I heard him last night, tonguing on a trail. He's gone out to hunt a fox."

His father said nothing, but he was looking at Jack in a way he had never looked before. Inwardly Jack felt a burning shame, and bit his lip to hold back the tears. His father's look told him plainly what Jeff was thinking. Good hounds, the only kind worth having, dedicate themselves wholeheartedly to the hunt and to their masters. It went without saying that a good master should be just as loyal to his hound. Thunder had been betrayed. When he heard the hound baying, Jack should have got up and gone out.

"Come on, Bub," was all his father said.

They stepped from the back porch into thirteen inches of undrifted snow. Still-falling snow clung to Jack's eyelashes, melted on his face, and coated his cap and jacket. He knew without being told that a strong hound at the peak of its powers could not possibly run very far in such fluffy snow. An eight-month-old puppy would do very well to make any headway at all.

The everlasting shame was that Thunder was somewhere out in the endless hills, alone. Jack had deserted him, and he must face that. Wanting to get a shovel so that he might clear paths, he started toward a tool shed built on the side of the house. He was halted by his father's voice.

"Never mind that now."

Jack looked around, surprised, but did not voice the question that was in his mind. Through the years he had learned to accept his father's leadership because his father always knew the best way to get things done. Side by side, plowing through snow that reached almost to their knees and fighting their way through drifts that came above their belts, they went to the barn. His father unlatched the door and they slid in quickly, before too much snow could blow in with them. Jack climbed into the haymow and began to fork down hay for the cattle and horses.

A stock barn on a winter's morning, and especially just after a heavy snow, is the most delightful place imaginable. Body heat of cattle and horses keeps it warm. There are a thousand different odors, most of them pleasant. The labor and fruits of the summer are there stored for the winter, and within them is a promise that spring and summer will come again. But this morning Jack felt no delight.

After feeding the stock, he gave the cattle their ration of grain and filled the horses' feed bins with oats. All must have fresh water, and when that had been taken care of Jack went back into the storm and made his way to the pigpen and chicken house. He fed and watered the pigs and chickens. When he returned to the barn, his father had finished milking.

Jack waited with heavy heart, for not until night would their tasks be ended. The snow was relentless. It had filled the roads and paths, and not until they were cleared would those at the Crowley farm be able to move freely. The bull-dozer blade would have to be hung on the tractor so his father could begin clearing roads while Jack shoveled paths.

But instead of starting toward the machine shed, Jeff said, "Wait here. I'll be back in a minute."

Jack sat down on an upended pail and waited miserably. He tried to tell himself that Thunder was not in trouble, but he knew that couldn't be. The snow was deep and getting deeper. Any puppy caught out in it, and all alone, was sure to be in plenty of trouble.

His father came back carrying a .22 rifle and two filled paper sacks. Jack looked up questioningly, and Jeff handed him one of the sacks.

"Stick it in your jacket, Bub."

"What is it?"

"Lunch. Come on."

He led the way to the shed where they stored axes, ropes, sleds, fishing tackle, and all the odds and ends that must be well tended but for which there was no room in the house. Jeff Crowley took his own snowshoes from the peg where they hung and nodded toward Jack's. Jack heart leaped and his hands trembled, for now he knew.

The creature comforts and immediate needs of every living thing on the farm had been taken care of. There was much work to be done and all of it was necessary, but all of it could wait while they went into the hills to hunt for a lost foxhound puppy. Jack looked gratefully at Jeff, but couldn't speak for the lump in his throat.

They laced on their snowshoes and went out into the fluffy snow. It was soft and yielding, and despite their gear they sank deep. Jack remembered that new snow, unless it is a light fall over a crust already formed, is never good snowshoeing. They were in for some hard work, but that didn't matter. They were going to look for Thunder.

From past experience, Jeff went directly to the tool shed where the three remaining chickens scratched contentedly in litter. With the practiced eye of an experienced woodsman he looked keenly about, and at once his glance found the feathers that were scattered around. Stooping, he studied the dirt floor.

"Look here," he exclaimed in surprise.

Jack knelt interestedly beside him. The floor of the shed was soft dirt, and Star had left his paw prints as plainly as they would have been imprinted on snow. But instead of the conventional paw mark of a fox, which is not unlike that of a dog, these had an extra toe on each front paw.

"A six-toed fox," Jeff said. "We'll know him if we see him."

He went to the door and looked into the storm. Jack waited. There were tracks in the shed, but blowing, drifting snow had long since wiped out any that might have been outside. There was no trail to tie them to the fleeing fox and the lost dog, but after a moment Jeff spoke confidently.

"He came from the south slope."

"How do you know?"

"The wind's been north since last night, and no hunting fox will travel any direction except into the wind. Thunder must have surprised him right after he caught the chicken, and for a while he would run the straightest course out of here."

"Wouldn't he drop the chicken?"

Jeff grinned. "I don't think so. Any fox hungry enough to come right into a shed and get a meal is likely to hold onto it as long as he can. Come on."

They bent their heads and plunged into the driving snow. There was not a single track, no sign whatever, to show where Thunder had gone. But Thunder would follow the fox and Jeff knew foxes. He was trying to think like a fox and in so doing to follow a course that a fox might have laid out.

Never hurrying, but never faltering, Jeff worked the probable trail. Snow flew about them, so that they could see only objects within a few feet, but Jeff Crowley knew every slope in the hills and every landmark. There was little danger of becoming lost.

They left the fields and entered the woods, where both stopped to rest. Heavy snow still fell but it was not cold, and both were sweating. Jeff spoke loudly above the wind.

"What time was it when you heard the hound tonguing?"

"I don't know exactly. I think it was early in the night."

Jeff nodded. "There wasn't so much snow then. They'd have run quite a way."

He cut around the hill, heading up a wooded valley. A half hour later he stopped again and pointed. In a wind-whipped aspen, whirled there by the wind and caught on a branch, was a single chicken feather. A warm glow began at the tip of Jack's toes and crept upward to the roots of his hair.

His father really knew his foxes and they were on the right trail. For the first time, Jack felt reasonably sure that they would find Thunder.

They quartered up the valley, always taking the easiest path and stopping frequently while Jeff concentrated on the trail he was trying to reconstruct. A burdened fox with a dog on his trail would choose the clearest path because he could run fastest on it. He would run around deep drifts instead of wasting time trying to plow through them. He would avoid steep cliffs and heavy thickets. His one idea would be to stay ahead of the hound.

It was past noon when, on the crest of a wooded hill, they stopped to eat their sandwiches. Brushing the snow from a boulder, they sat down and rested. Then Jeff started down the opposite side of the hill into a copse of shriveled beech brush. He went slowly, taking time to look and listen, and always trying to choose the path where a fox might have run.

In mid-afternoon the wind was cut by a different sound. A quarter of a mile away it was, across the sloping nose of a hillock and toward the mouth of a wooded draw. It came again, the melodious baying of a foxhound. Jeff swerved toward the draw.

A little way up it, hungry and exhausted, but still fighting through snow that rolled over his back, they found him. Thunder's tongue lolled, his sides heaved, and his strength was almost gone. But he was still pushing himself through the snow, searching for the scent that had somehow eluded him. He had lost the fox, but the deep, true instincts of a born trailing hound told him that it could not be forever lost. If only he kept seeking, he would find it again.

Thunder sank down in the snow and wagged a whip-thin tail. He smiled with his eyes, but wriggled in protest when Jeff knelt beside him and cradled him in his arms. A moment later he was resting across Jeff's shoulders, where he finally sighed and relaxed. Jack looked wonderingly at his father.

There was about him no anger or irritation because he had lost a whole day, but only the satisfaction of a job well done. A hunter himself, Jeff knew and understood a fine hunting hound. As they headed back to the farmhouse, he turned to Jack.

"You picked yourself a real hound, Bub."

Chapter 3  The Crust

At first the chase had been a frightening one for Star. The fox had never before had a hound on his trail, and the dog's excited tonguing had been a coldly terrifying sound. At the same time, it gave wings to Star's flying black paws. It did not rouse him to panic, so that he even thought of dropping the chicken. That meal had been perilously won and not lightly would Star abandon it.

The snow held him back, and because the hound was longer-legged, he could run faster. Thunder had narrowed the gap between them to a few hundred feet when, as a desperate measure, Star leaped to the trunk of a huge pine that had fallen years ago.

The tree was dead, all the bark was gone, and only spikes of limbs thrust out at different angles.

Star leaped to the tree trunk because the brisk wind had blown it snow-free and he might gain a second of precious time if he did not have to travel in snow. He raced up the trunk and leaped from the far end of the tree back into the snow. Again he resumed his floundering course, listening for the hound as he ran.

He heard the dog baying more faintly, and knew by the sound that Thunder had fallen much farther behind. He was lingering around the fallen tree, tonguing steadily, and Star gained a safe lead while at the same time he remembered what he had done. There was a break in his trail where he had left the snow to leap onto the tree, and apparently broken trails deceived dogs. Star could not know that a ruse as simple as the one he had employed would not have halted an experienced hound for more than a second, but Thunder was a puppy who had as much to learn about running foxes as Star must learn about avoiding hounds.

Star's fear lessened, and he actually began to enjoy the chase. There was within him a pronounced spirit of mischief and a real capacity for enjoying games. Foiling the hound became a game.

The next time he came to a fallen tree he sprang up and ran along it, but that time Thunder paused only momentarily. He, too, was learning. Instead of casting aimlessly about, he went directly to the fallen tree, picked up the trail, and followed it. Star did not worry.

His was the agile brain of a red fox, and he had already taught himself that a broken trail can halt a hound. When Star came to a little runlet of water that purled blackly between heaped snowbanks he leaped in, followed the runlet to the spring that was its source, and once more plunged into the snow. He ran another half mile and discovered suddenly that he couldn't even hear the dog.

Star slowed to a walk, then stopped beneath a big hemlock. He dropped the chicken and placed one paw on it, as though to hold it down and mark it as his property. His tongue lolled like a hot, panting dog's. While the snow drove about, he turned to face the back trail as he listened and tested the air with his nose. There was still no indication that the hound was on his trail.

Star crouched in the snow and held the chicken down with both front paws. With his sharp teeth he carefully plucked the feathers from its breast and shook his head to cast aside those that stuck to his teeth. The wind whirled them away, blowing one into a nearby aspen where it hung on a twig.

He had scarcely started his meal when, faint but very clear, the wind brought to him the hound's rolling bays. Star stopped eating and stood erect, pinning the chicken down with a front paw. Beyond any doubt, Thunder had worked out the trail and was again on the way.

Star picked up the partly eaten chicken and trotted on. His fear was gone, and he had a mounting confidence that he could continue to evade this dog. He did not bother to run fast, but saved his strength for any spurts that might be needed.

He ran up more fallen trees, even though this maneuver no longer baffled the hound. Star traveled in such places only because he did not have to fight the deepening snow when he did so. When he came to another little trickle of water he jumped in and ran for a hundred yards through it. Emerging, he ran a little way and again waited.

He was very confident that the hound would again be delayed, and he was right. But this time Thunder did not take nearly as long to work the trail out and discover for himself what Star had done. His ringing voice woke the wilderness as he came on.

Morning broke, slanted into noon, and still the chase went on. Star rested when he could, snatched a few more mouthfuls from the chicken when he rested, and ran on again when Thunder's voice roused him. The hound, who never had a chance to rest, was tiring. But as long as he could possibly follow it, he had no thought of abandoning the trail.

The deepening snow broke the scent as effectively as anything Star had done. Only wisps of scent filtered through the snow, and Thunder was so weary now that his fastest speed was a snail's pace. Star heard him give tongue, faintly. The fox waited, and after a bit he heard the dog no more.

Star knew nothing of what had taken place, that Jeff and Jack Crowley had found Thunder and were taking him home. He knew only that he could no longer hear the dog. The fox walked on, and after another half hour had passed he decided that the dog would come no more.

He wanted two things now, to get out of the storm and to finish his meal. Carrying the chicken, he struck a slanting course toward some rock bluffs that reared at the base of a hill. Threading his way among a litter of huge boulders that thrust out of the snow, he came at last to the bluffs.

He knew the place well. The boulders were honeycombed with numerous burrows where striped chipmunks lived, and often Star and Brush had hunted them. Just beyond, leaning against the base of the bluffs, was a huge flat stone and behind that a fissure where a peevish porcupine made its home. Star slipped behind the leaning stone and for the first time was out of the storm. With his keen nose he investigated the fissure.

The porcupine was sleeping on a ledge. A grunting, complaining old beast, it lived in the fissure whenever it was not gnawing one of the yellow birches that sprouted among the aspens. The fissure also sheltered another refugee, a white weasel that had come to hunt chipmunks and had stayed to rest. Unhesitatingly, Star entered.

The porcupine awoke when Star passed it, gritted its teeth, and grunted softly. Star paid no attention. He knew better than to go near the porcupine. A sudden flip of its tail or a mis-step on his part might puncture his flesh with some of the twenty thousand little spears carried by this armed beast of the wilderness.

Star walked toward the rear of the gloomy fissure, laid the chicken down, again holding it with his front paws, and shook himself prodigiously. Fine spray flew from his wet fur. Star shook himself a second time, but less vigorously. With meticulous care he licked each of his four paws in turn and swung his head to lick his flanks. His grooming complete, he stretched full length to enjoy his often-interrupted meal.

He ate only part of the chicken, but kept his paws on the part that remained. The weasel was still in the cave and he knew weasels. They were blood-thirsty, vicious things, and a hungry weasel would attack almost anything in order to get the food it wanted. The chicken very close to his nose, Star stretched out for a nap.

His was a light slumber, so delicately balanced that even while he slept a part of him remained awake. He knew every time the porcupine grunted, and when the weasel slipped out in the raging storm to hunt. When the weasel returned, it was in an ugly mood, its little eyes red, angry coals. Though it had burrowed into the snow for two hours, seeking anything at all to eat, it had found nothing.

The weasel snarled at Star as it passed and the fox grimaced back. He had no liking for weasels, mink, marten, or fisher, all creatures that exude a powerful musk, but he was not particularly afraid of any of them. Star resumed his nap, and when he awakened he finished the rest of the chicken.

The roaring of the wind came as a muted sound into the fissure, and told of the storm still raging. Walking to the opening, the porcupine looked out and chattered senselessly to itself. Not liking what it saw, it came back in, scrambled up to the ledge, and went to sleep again. Nothing wanted to move around outside as long as the storm raged.

The next morning snow stopped falling and the skies cleared. Star went to the opening of the fissure and looked out. With the end of the storm the weather had turned very cold. In a clear blue sky, the sun was a round ball that seemed to have lost its fire. Frost rimed the hardwoods, and trees penetrated by creeping frost filled the forest with noises like the blasting of so many shotguns.

Soft, feathery snow lay thirty inches deep all over the wilderness. Though the weather had not been cold while the snow fell, it had been cold enough to keep the snow fairly dry so that no crust had formed. Star went out in it, but after a minute he turned back. All his energy was needed just to travel and he could see, hear, and smell almost nothing. In spite of the fact that he had eaten all the chicken and was hungry again, there was little prospect of successful hunting in snow like this. Star went back into the fissure.

Last night the place had been comfortably warm, but now it was very cold and frost glazed the walls. Star sought a place between two boulders and curled up, warming his paws with his body and curling his fluffy tail around exposed eyes and nose, which kept them from the danger of freezing.

As usual he slept lightly, aware of what went on about him, and awakened when the grunting old porcupine waddled to the fissure's mouth. Leaving a broad trail behind him, the squat, powerful creature plunged through the snow to the nearest yellow birch. It climbed the tree, settled itself comfortably on a branch, and began to gnaw bark.

After an hour, again driven by hunger, Star followed. He stood for a moment beneath the leaning stone, then followed the furrow the porcupine had made and went to the tree. He looked at a flicker of motion in another tree and saw six chickadees flitting about.

Star eyed them wistfully. The chickadees were tiny things, scarcely a mouthful, but the fox was

hungry enough to eat almost anything. He knew
that he could not get the chickadees because they
were in a tree and he could not climb trees. For a
moment he watched them dart industriously about,
then turned his attention to the fat old porcupine. It
did not glance down. Underneath its quills was
thick fur and tough skin that defied cold weather,
and the quills protected it from most enemies. The
porcupine calmly devoted itself to eating bark.

Again Star plunged into the snow and sank almost
out of sight. Half a dozen leaps carried him forward,
while snow sifted into his sensitive nose and eyes.
He sneezed and turned back to the fissure.

The weasel was coming out. A foot-long, whip-
thin creature, the weasel sprang agilely to a crack in
the rocks and hovered near it without entering. Its
jaws parted in a snarl and the black tip of its white
tail twitched like an angry cat's as it glared at Star.
The fox made a single sidewise leap that carried him
toward the crack and the weasel slipped like a white
shadow into it. Star, who had known that the weasel
could elude him but who had felt like chasing it
anyhow, went back to his bed and slept. He would
just have to bear his hunger until he could do something about it.

The porcupine did not return, and when night
lowered over the wilderness Star trotted inquisi-
tively out to see where it was. Stars glittered
through sparkling, frost-filled air and a pale moon

seemed to reflect merciless cold. It was far below zero, but the porcupine slept placidly in the yellow birch. Having eaten as much as it wished, it did not even move when Star paused beneath the tree.

It was a still and frozen world, with even the wind silent. The wan moon, shining through leafless trees, outlined them against deep and unruffled snow. With no cheerful chickadees to loan assurance that spring was sure to come again, the night wilderness in winter was a dead place. Star went back to the fissure.

All night long the cold held sway, and all the next day. Once more the weasel went forth to hunt and again it failed. Driven to madness by hunger, it went berserk.

When it came back into the fissure it did so at a dead run. Its little eyes were burning, its jaws framed a snarl. Straight at the fox it ran, and when it was three feet away its body arched into the air as it attacked.

Not knowing what to expect, Star dodged backward. He brought up against the rocks, and for a moment was afraid, the attack was so unexpected and the weasel so furious. If Star could have run he would have, but there was no place to go. The weasel sank its fangs into his lip and dangled with only its hind paws on the ground.

The startled fox flipped his head to shake his tormentor off, but so fierce was the weasel's grip that a

section of Star's lip tore out. Scrambling with all
four paws, the piece of Star's lip still tight in its
teeth, the weasel was tossed toward the roof of the
fissure. Star dashed forward, snapped, and caught
the falling creature before it touched the ground. As
it died, the weasel filled the fissure with rank scent.

Star licked his bleeding lip and shook his head.
Like all foxes he was fastidious. The weasel's musk,
not unlike the scent of a skunk, filled his mouth and
clung to his jaws. Trotting to the mouth of the fissure, Star filled his mouth with fresh, clean snow.
He closed his jaws, chewing the snow until it was
compressed into ice and grinding that with his
teeth. Again and again he cleansed his mouth with
snow, but the weasel's musk still lingered.

Going back, Star sniffed at his dead enemy, and
grimaced. Any meat, almost any food, was to be
preferred to this. But Star was ravenous. He sliced
the weasel's skin with expert jaws, pinned the slight
body beneath his front paws, and pulled the skin
off. Chopping out the tail section, where the musk
glands were located, he ate the weasel's warm flesh
without chewing it at all. Then he lay down and
used his tongue to stanch blood that dripped from
his lacerated lip.

A few hours later, the weather began to change.

The sun rose in a still cloudless sky, but this
morning there was warmth in its glow. For a brief
time the cold was beaten back. Inside the fissure

the frost glazing melted, and water streaked the walls. The fluffy snow wilted, and within a few hours its depth was decreased by six inches. Snow water crept over the ice that locked streams and ponds in its frozen grip. But it was only a temporary respite. The cold came back again, the inside of the fissure became sheathed with ice, and the water on the streams and ponds froze hard.

Just before nightfall Star left his bed to trot out of the fissure. When he walked down the trail that the porcupine had broken, his black paws found ridges of ice. He came to the yellow birch and looked up at the porcupine, which was busy girdling another branch. Venturing to the end of the trail that he himself had broken, Star leaped to the top of the snow.

He didn't know what to expect, and because he did not he slipped. Each of his four paws skidded in a different direction, so that for a moment he lay spread-eagled on the snow. Lying still, Star tried to determine what this was and how it could be handled. When he tried to get up, he only slipped again. Melted by the warm spell, the snow had frozen again and formed a crust that was as hard and as slippery as ice.

The next time he tried to get up, Star did so cautiously, gathering his paws beneath him and relaxing his body. He stood erect, took a few cautious steps, and found his legs once more. Walking on a smooth crust required a special technique of its own.

As soon as Star mastered it his walk became a trot, then gave way to the swift undulating pace which a red fox uses to flow over the ground. Once he learned to stand up on it, the crust presented a perfectly smooth path. For a mile Star ran as swiftly as he could. His muscles and sinews were young and supple, and all the while he had been in the fissure, a prisoner of the storm, he had had no chance to exercise them. Now he could, and he took fullest advantage of the opportunity. Star leaped clear over a laurel bush just to prove that he could do it, and then ran around the bush three times. His excess energy burned up, he settled down to the business of hunting.

Prowling through a swamp, he saw numerous deer. Usually the deer didn't yard, or gather in a place where a herd might safely spend the winter, until January or later. The fierce storm had driven this herd into the swamp, and from now until spring they would stay there, living on the white cedar and other forage they could reach. Because they had yarded very early, the forage in the swamp would be depleted before any new spring foliage took its place and the herd was due for a hard winter.

Star walked through the yard, following paths that the deer had beaten. They scarcely moved aside as he trotted among them. In a spirit of mischief he dashed at a fawn and watched the alarmed creature skip away. But when he tried the same thing with a craggy-horned buck, the buck turned and shook its antlers at him. Star dodged aside, and watched with interest a deer that had left the yard and was walking through the deep snow.

Hard enough to support a small animal, the crust was not hard enough to bear the weight of a full-grown deer's sharp hoofs. With every step the floundering animal broke through. Freeing its legs after a struggle, it advanced another step or two. The deer sank into a deep drift, thrashed furiously to get out, and Star watched hopefully. Maybe the deer would be unable to get out of the drift and would die in it. But a moment later she freed herself and fought back into one of the yard's beaten paths.

Disappointed, Star left the yard. There was nothing whatever for him to eat in it. He could catch a deer, but he could not kill one after he caught it. The wintering herd had eaten all the ground browse and left nothing that would interest a fox.

Again on the crust, Star trotted easily along. He stopped in his tracks as the scent of nesting mice drifted to his nostrils, and scratched at the snow through which the scent came. But it was very faint and far off, and Star's raking nails only scratched long marks in the snow. He gave up because of the crust's hardness and because he could not locate the mice exactly anyhow.

Ten minutes later, while prowling through a laurel thicket, he caught a ground-roosting grouse at the base of a frosty aspen. Not often were grouse so unwise, but this one was and he paid with his life for his foolishness. Star plucked the bird and stretched out on the snow to eat it.

He was half through the meal when suddenly he stopped eating and tensed himself. A snarl curled his upper lip and wrinkled his nose. Bristling, he waited.

Clearly outlined in the moon's wan light, another fox came into the laurel. She was a slim young vixen, a spring pup of the same age as Star. Her fur rippled smoothly as she halted ten feet away. Star growled warningly and hastily gulped the rest of the grouse. She did not move while he ground the bones between his teeth, so after the grouse was finished, Star rose.

In the cold night he faced her, unwilling to share his food but entirely ready to be friendly. When he moved toward her she whirled and ran, but she did not call forth all her wonderful speed. Without effort Star reached her side. All her hair fluffed so that she seemed twice as big as she really was, Vixen crouched on the snow. Her teeth snapped an inch from Star's face. She could have cut him had she wanted to, but she, too, was lonely and had no wish to hurt him.

Star's tail wagged slowly, like a dog's, as he

sniffed her nose. A faint trace of rabbit scent lingered about her mouth and jaws; she, too, had eaten. Star made a little forward spring and Vixen sprang backward. Side by side they whirled over the crust. Stopping, they wrestled like playful pups.

Within neither was there any desire for a mate. Both were too young to feel such urges and the mating season for foxes was still weeks away. They were merely two lonely youngsters who were perfectly satisfied to have each other's company. Vixen trotted smoothly toward the high country and Star paced contentedly at her side. When they were tired, they lay up together in a laurel thicket.

They left the thicket when they were hungry, and in broad daylight went forth to hunt. Like all their kind, they regulated themselves by their own desires and needs. The time to sleep was when they were sleepy and the time to hunt when they were hungry. Only where there is heavy hunting and trapping pressure upon them do foxes range exclusively at night.

The crust made a perfect highway and they could sense no enemies abroad. They headed toward a patch of brush where cottontail rabbits lived and Vixen left Star. He ranged into the brush, and didn't even have to put his keen nose to the ground in order to know there was food about. Though they had been stormbound, like everything else, now the cottontails were out in force. They ranged at will throughout the thicket to wherever tender twigs and brush were found, and were not confined to paths and runways. Star struck a fresh trail and coursed it.

He flew easily along the scent he had chosen, in no special hurry. The cottontail he pursued might take to the earth or it might decide to outrun him. If the former, Star could do nothing except abandon the trail and select another. But if the cottontail decided to run after Star sighted it, then he would call on all his reserves of speed and whether or not he caught his prey would depend on which could run faster.

The trail freshened and Star leaped along it. He burst around a squat, scrub hemlock to find Vixen with the rabbit he had trailed. Cutting around the hemlock, it had run right into her. A bubbling snarl sputtered in her throat. She watched Star from the corners of her eyes, then turned and trotted twenty feet away. Lying down, she began to eat.

When she had all she wanted, Vixen rose to lick her jaws and did not snarl again when Star came to get what remained. It was not a choice selection because Vixen had taken all the best for herself, nor was it enough to still Star's hunger. But it was food, and quite by accident they had discovered a new way of hunting. Two foxes, one in ambush and one coursing, were much more effective than just one.

That night two inches of fresh, new snow piled itself on top of the crust. Vixen strayed away while Star played with a piece of stick. Clutching the stick in his jaws, he flipped his head and sent his plaything high in the air. Then he leaped forward to catch it before it struck the snow. Or sometimes he let it come down and, rearing, pounced on it with his front paws.

Tiring of the game, Star sought the lee of a mossy log, curled up, protected his eyes and nose with his tail, and slept. With morning he left his bed, both hungry and lonesome. Because he wanted company more than he did food, he worked down the ridges to see if he could find Vixen.

He was going around the point of a hill when the morning silence was broken by the tonguing of two hounds on a trail. Star leaped to the top of a snow-covered boulder so he could hear better. He knew by their voices that neither dog was Thunder, but he remembered that chase very well.

Terrifying at first, it had become sport as the chase progressed. There had been real pleasure in foiling the dog by breaking his trail. Star danced in nervous anticipation, for the chase was coming his way. Presently he saw Vixen, whose trail the hounds were on, streaking among the trees.

After she had gone, Star jumped from the rock and waited until he saw the hounds. They were blueticks, smaller than Thunder, with a streak of mongrel in them. At the same instant both dogs saw Star and their voices blended in an ecstatic frenzy.

Star waited another split second, then flashed away.

Chapter 4  Haunt Fox

Dade Matson lived all alone in a three-room cabin at the mouth of a wooded valley known as Hungry Hollow. Nobody could remember the time when Dade had not been a woods prowler, and that's all he had ever been. In summer he roamed the forest with a sack over his shoulder and hunted medicinal roots. In the fall and winter he hunted and trapped furs. His whole living he took out of the forests and waters around him.

The hard-working farmers of the valley didn't blame Dade for living as he did. Given the opportunity, some of them would cheerfully have sold their farms and retreated to a three-room cabin. But they wouldn't have lived as Dade did, and they wouldn't have had his unsavory reputation. It was not that he ever did anything so very bad, or anything that most of his neighbors at one time or another hadn't done themselves. But what the rest did in moments of weakness or stress, Dade practiced habitually.

There was no doubt that his table was well supplied with game and fish taken in or out of season. If there was a bounty on any beast, Dade never hesitated to kill it whether or not its fur was prime. It was suspected that he used poison to kill fur bearers and certainly he poached beavers. But no game warden ever caught him because Dade knew every inch of the territory he hunted and trapped and was as woods-wise as a trap-pinched coyote.

In the eyes of the farmers, none of this added up to serious crime. There was just something about Dade himself that set him apart and marked him as a cold and hard man, one to be watched. Though it was common practice in the valley for one man to help another, with no thought of compensation, everything Dade did had a price tag attached. He cared nothing for anyone or anything except himself, and possibly his two foxhounds.

On this wintry day he strode homeward as dusk fell. His shotgun was in his hands and the tired hounds were at his heel, but no fox hung over his shoulder. He chained the dogs to their kennels, fed them, ate his own meal, and for a while sat staring at the darkened window.

After a bit he put on his cap and jacket and walked over the crust to the Crowley farm. Jack Crowley answered the door.

"Hello, Dade."

Without waiting for an invitation, for that was the way of the valley, Dade stamped snow from his rubber pacs and came into the warm kitchen. Jeff Crowley put aside the magazine he was reading and Jack's mother looked up from her mending.

"Have a cup of coffee, Dade?"

"Thanks, I will."

As he sipped the cup of steaming hot coffee she gave him, Jeff asked, "How are things?"

"Queer," Dade stated. "Queer enough, Jeff. I was up in the hills today with my dogs. I think we got a ha'nt fox up there."

Jack sat silently in his chair, but paid rapt attention. A "haunt" fox was an especially elusive one, a beast with ghost-like qualities. In all the lore of the valley there had been no more than four such, and it was vastly exciting to have another.

As interested as his son, Jeff asked, "Where'd you find him, Dade?"

"I didn't. He found me. I was up in Spruce Gully when the hounds cut a fresh track. From the way the fox acted and run I took it for a yearlin' vixen. I figured she'd circle through the gap at the head of the gully and I cut around. Would of got her there, too, but all of a sudden the dogs raised a fuss. It sounded like they'd caught a fox on the ground, and I run down as fast as I could so they wouldn't tear it too much and spoil the pelt."

Deliberately Dade sipped his coffee. He had an interested audience, and it was no part of a storyteller's technique to spoil everything by revealing the climax too soon.

"What happened next?" Jeff prompted him.

"Well, I got down and saw by tracks in the snow that my hounds hadn't caught the vixen at all, and I found out why. She's got a mate, a ha'nt fox, and he cut in ahead of the dogs. He must have waited until they were almost right on top of him before he made up his mind to run. A dog fox will take hounds away from his vixen when she's pushed hard."

"I know."

"After the fox tore away with my dogs right behind him, I took a closer look at his tracks. In all my time in the woods I never did see such a fox track; there's an extra toe on each front paw. I figured, 'Well, Mr. Bigfoot, you wanted those hounds on yourself and you got 'em. Now let's see if you're smart enough to dodge a dose of number four shot.' Now that I knew it was a dog fox tryin' to take hounds away from his vixen, I changed my way of huntin'. I figured he'd run straight away for a piece and prob'ly wouldn't circle back to where she was."

Dade took another prolonged sip of coffee, while Jack waited breathlessly. The fox that had stolen the chicken, and later lost Thunder in the snow, had an extra toe on each front paw. It *must* be the same one.

"A fox runnin' straight away," Dade continued, "would first get far enough so the dogs wouldn't go back to his vixen, then he'd try to lose the hounds. I figured this one'd try it in the left fork of Bear Paw Crick; that seemed about right. He'd also run through the notch at the head of the valley, 'stead of climbin' over all them snow-covered rocks. So I hustled me up to the notch and hid in the laurel where I could get a good, wide sweep. Pretty soon, sure enough, I heard the dogs a-streakin' along. They were just footin' the breeze."

Dade finished his coffee, then resumed his tale. "Right through the laurel them hounds tore, not twenty yards from where I was standin'! That fox hadn't come through before I was set! So he came afterwards, right under my eyes. Why didn't I see him?"

Jeff said, "You must have missed seeing him when he came."

"I could of," Dade admitted. "I could of done that, but wait until you hear the rest. Like I thought, the fox ran straight for Bear Paw Crick. I was mad anyhow on account I hadn't got him in the notch, so I run down to the crick to find out what was what. The hounds was runnin' this way and that, and like to drive themselves crazy, and where was the fox?"

"Where?" Jack breathed.

"Wish I could tell you that, I just wish I could. There's a lashin' big spruce right at the edge of the crick there, and the fox tracks ended a full six feet from that spruce!"

"The trail ended?" Jeff questioned.

"It ended!" Dade declared.

"Was Bear Paw Creek frozen?" Jeff asked.

"No. It's free runnin'."

"Maybe he jumped into the creek?"

Dade snorted. "A fox jump thirty feet or more?"

"Did he get into the tree?"

"Red foxes don't climb trees."

Jeff said slowly, "I've known them to. Of course a red fox doesn't climb like a gray, but they will use trees to break a trail. Does that spruce have any low-hanging branches?"

"Yeh. It does. But the dogs would of smelled him if he'd gone into the tree."

"Some dogs would and some wouldn't."

"Mine would," Dade declared stiffly. "Anyhow, I looked in the tree and he wasn't there. I tell you it's a ha'nt fox and the man who gets him will have to be a real fox hunter!"

Jeff's eyes were twinkling. "You don't think he can dodge a charge of shot?"

His temper already roused by what he considered Jeff's slighting reference to his dogs, Dade flared. "Nope. He can't. One of these days I'll bring his pelt around and prove it! Thanks for the coffee!"

Dade went out the door into the winter's night. Grinning faintly, Jeff watched him go. Jack looked questioningly at his father.

"What do you think really happened?"

"Just about what Dade said. He would have read the signs right. Dade can do that, even if he doesn't have too much imagination."

"But—a fox just can't take off like a bird."

Jeff's eyes were dreamy as he thought of the past fox hunts he himself had enjoyed. "There are stupid foxes just as there are stupid people, but on the average, when it comes to brains and deception, they know more tricks than a professional magician. Put a man and a hound, or even a pack of hounds, against a red fox and the odds still favor the fox. That's why, if you aren't hunting for money, fox hunting is so much fun."

"How do you think the fox got past Dade without being seen?"

"My guess is that he wasn't even looking for a man, and that he was almost on Dade before he knew it. What choice did it leave him? The hounds were behind and Dade was in front. He used his head and sneaked past. It would be hard for even Dade to see a sneaking fox in thick laurel. He had expected a running animal."

Jack thought about this, and about something else. This was Wednesday, and it was only two more days until Saturday. Maybe Thunder would be able to run Saturday. Furthermore, the fox was marked. An extra toe on each front paw would definitely prove him the haunt fox, the animal that had foiled Dade Matson and his hounds. Just suppose . . .

"How do you suppose he broke his trail?" Jack asked.

Jeff shook his head. "You'll have to ask the fox that. My guess is that the spruce had something to do with it. It's true that red foxes don't climb trees, but this one could have jumped into a lower branch, climbed along it, and climbed out another branch until he was over the creek. Then he wouldn't have to do anything except drop into the water."

Jack went out on the back porch to make sure Thunder was there, and the black and tan puppy padded over to get his evening's caress. His paws, left raw and bleeding from his long chase after Star, were not entirely healed and he walked with a pronounced limp. But there were two full days between now and Saturday.

That night another two inches of snow fell, and the next day the cold wave continued. Examining

Thunder's paws, Jack found that there were still raw and chafed places on them. Hopefully he massaged them with lard and even thought of making four leather moccasins. Jeff advised him not to. A hunting hound is a working dog who must often venture into dangerous places. At all times he needs free use of his feet, and moccasins might impede his running. Also, unless they were very expertly made and fitted, they could do more harm than good. It was best to leave Thunder as he was.

It was not yet daylight when Jack awakened Saturday morning. He slipped an exploring hand from beneath the heavy quilt that covered him, found his underwear and socks where he had left them on a chair, and without rising from the warm bed he wriggled out of his pajamas and into his underwear and socks. He sprang out of bed, hurriedly pulled his trousers on, and left his unbuttoned shirt hanging loosely around his slim chest and stomach. Carrying his shoes, he ran out of his cold room and downstairs into the warm kitchen.

Jeff was at the kitchen sink, washing his face and hands in a bowl of warm water, and Jack's mother was preparing breakfast. Jack buttoned his shirt and sat down to put his shoes on, and when he bent over his trousers tightened uncomfortably. His mother glanced around and saw it.

"Are your trousers tight?"

"Sort of."

"You grow like a spring colt," his mother sighed. "I just bought those for you a few months ago and they're hardly worn. Well, Pete Mason will be able to use them and we'll get you some more in Carneyville today."

Jack said nothing because there was nothing to say. He had one good suit which he wore to all social functions, but otherwise all his clothing was chosen with an eye to strict utility. His trousers must serve both for school and for work around the farm. Long ago Jack had decided that what he really wanted was a pair of peg-top hunting breeches, the sort that hugged the leg and fitted snugly into a hunting boot, but he knew that he had little chance of getting them.

His father had such a pair of breeches, but they hung in the closet most of the time. Jack had long eyed them wistfully and knew that, with a little taking in at the belt, he could wear them. But Jeff had pronounced ideas about who was and who was not big enough to wear his breeches and no fourteen-year-old would qualify.

Jack washed, and while his mother was finishing the meal he slipped outside. A ghost shape in the blackness, Thunder came trotting up. He wriggled ecstatically under Jack's soothing hand, and pushed his cold nose against his master's thigh. Jack picked up one of Thunder's paws, stroked it gently, and the hound did not wince. He might be able to run, but it was still only a couple of days since his pads had been raw. Jack stood indecisively. He wanted to go on a fox hunt, but not if it would hurt Thunder.

He went back into the house and took his place at the breakfast table. His parents were discussing their trip to Carneyville, where they went twice a month to do shopping. They always left right after the chores were finished and never came back until early evening. Jack could go with them or not, just as he chose, and quite often he preferred to stay on the farm. It was nice to have a whole day with no adult supervision.

Jack fed Thunder, then went to the barn with his father. The black and tan hound trailed them out and curled up comfortably beside a bale of straw while Jack forked down hay for the cattle, and fed and watered the stock. It was not until the chores were almost finished that Jack appealed to Jeff for help with his problem.

"Do you think Thunder can run today?"

Jeff nibbled his lower lip and looked at the hound. For a moment he said nothing. Then he turned back to his chores.

"Thunder's your dog, Bub."

Jack knew that it would be useless to say any more. He wasn't big enough to wear Jeff's breeches, and wouldn't be until he could make his own decisions. Thunder left the bale of straw and wagged up to sniff at a crevice in which mice were hiding. Jack noticed that he no longer limped.

When they were through, a thin and uncertain daylight had come. Jeff backed the farm truck out of its shed, ran it down to the house, and parked beside the kitchen door. Dressed for winter, Jack's mother came out of the house and stood beside the truck. Jeff called to him from the driver's seat.

"You going?"

"No thanks. I'll stay here."

"There's cold pork and milk in the icebox," his mother said as she took her place beside Jeff. "Make yourself a sandwich at noon and we'll have a hot meal tonight."

"I will."

"Keep out of mischief," his father said as he put the truck in low gear and drove slowly down the frozen lane toward the plowed highway.

Jack stood with his hand on Thunder's head and for a moment wished that he had gone along. If he had, he would not now have to decide whether or not to run Thunder. He looked at the snow-blanketed hills rising around the farm, and at the thin forest covering them. The forest always looked thin in winter, when the only green showing was that of a few shrubs and evergreens. In summer, when all the trees and bushes were in leaf, the woods looked very thick.

Jack's heart beat fast and hard, so that he imagined he could hear it. The hills were there, the snow was right, and foxes would be running the snow. Suddenly he knew what he could do, and it wasn't as though he *had* to let Thunder run a fox. He could keep him on leash, but at least they could go see if there were any foxes. Jack went into the house, took his shot gun from its rack, broke the breech, and glanced through the spotless bore.

There was no need for snowshoes since the crust still held, and the fresh snow on top of it was not deep enough to impede them. At the end of a short chain, Thunder paced contentedly beside his master.

They passed through the fields, and Jack read in the snow the story of other passers-by. Cottontail rabbits had played and skipped about. There were delicate traceries where mice had traveled back and forth, and a suddenly broken rabbit's trail. Only there was no mystery as to how these tracks had ended. On both sides of the trail's end were marks where wing tips had brushed the snow. A cruising great horned owl had swooped and snatched the rabbit.

Leaving the fields, they entered the woods and Jack stopped to look with interest at a line of huge cat tracks. He recognized them as a wild cat's paw prints and knew they were fresh. Stub had prowled here last night, hungrily thinking of the farm. But, unlike Star, he had lacked the courage to raid it. Stub's tracks curved up the hill and toward the deeper wilderness.

Thunder raised his head, stood for a second, and sniffed prodigiously. A happy little whine broke from him and for the first time he strained at the leash. Jack felt a warm excitement and broke into a trot. Thunder hadn't even sniffed at the rabbit tracks, the meadow mouse tracings, or Stub's scent. He was born to hunt just one thing, and Jack knew that the next tracks they ran across would be those of a fox.

They found the trail about halfway between the farm and the summit of the hill. Clear and fresh in the snow the paw prints were, so the fox must have made them about the time Jeff and Jack were doing the chores. They were not the marks of the six-toed beast, the Haunt Fox, but a red fox had certainly walked here within the past couple of hours.

Thunder came suddenly and gloriously alive. Heedless of the choking collar, he pulled Jack along the tracks. The hound snuffled loudly and his over-hanging jaws quivered as the odor of his natural enemy set his brain on fire. His scraping paws left scratch marks in the snow.

Jack twined his hand in the taut chain even though, for the moment, he was unable to make up his mind. Then he could no longer help himself. Thunder had chased the Haunt Fox, the ghost

animal, and had gained his sore paws on that hunt.
This fox was just an ordinary creature. Holding the
shotgun in the crook of his arm, Jack grasped Thunder's collar and held the straining hound to get slack
in the chain. With his free hand he unsnapped the
chain and Thunder sprang forward.

From Thunder's throat, a rolling, musical roar
floated out into the frosty air. Thunder bayed again,
and again. Then he tongued smoothly and evenly,
and his voice blended with its own echoes to form a
rhythmic cadence. It was hunter's music, and to the
fox hunter no other song is ever as stirring.

Running hard, Thunder went out of sight. For a
second Jack wished that he could recall the hound,
but at the same time he knew that he could not.
Thunder had never been taught to respond to a
hunting horn; the hunters in these hills did not use
them. It was useless to whistle or call, for Thunder
was hopelessly beyond hearing. Jack knew that he
must act.

The fox hunter's art, as practiced by hill men who
hunt with one or two hounds, has nothing whatever
to do with red coats and galloping horses. The lone
hunter must know his game and be able to think like
a fox. His strategy is to outwit his quarry. Guided
only by what he knows of foxes and their ways, and
the voice of his tonguing hound, the hunter tries to
intercept the fox, to be where the fox will be in a
half hour, or two hours, or four hours. Then, if he

does everything exactly right, the hunter usually gets one shot at the flashing red streak which is a running fox.

While a full minute ticked past, Jack listened to Thunder's tonguing. His steady tones quickened and rose to an excited pitch, so Jack knew that he had jumped his quarry from a bed. Probably the fox had bedded in a patch of laurel about halfway up a valley that cut around the other side.

Thunder's tonguing became normal and Jack knew that he was leveling out to run. Jack tried to think clearly.

The running fox, he decided, would not cross the valley and climb the hill on the opposite side. The fact that he had bedded in the valley was within itself indicative that he had made a kill in or near it. His tracks were very fresh, therefore he must have hunted all night long before catching anything to eat. No doubt he had traveled a considerable distance. He had been heading toward the valley, so his home territory, the range he hunted most, must therefore be on this side of it. The chances were that he would circle soon and come back up this slope.

Having made his decision, Jack acted on it. He ran as hard as he could up the hill, toward the head of the valley. He took a stance in a patch of aspens and tried to control his labored breathing; the uphill run had left him gasping. As soon as he had caught his breath, he knew he had made a mistake.

Thunder's voice told him that the fox was coming nearer, but not through the aspens. Instead, his course was taking him into a thin patch of hemlocks that lay like a green ribbon up and down the hillside, about three hundred yards from where Jack was standing. Too late Jack ran toward the hemlocks. He called and whistled, but the steadily tonguing hound ran on.

The fox had done what a wise fox will do. Though his initial course would have taken him through the aspens, he knew about hunters with shotguns. Because the hemlocks furnished more cover, he had taken advantage of it.

Jack reached the hemlocks to find two trails. The hound's was spotted with blood; obviously Thunder's scarcely healed paws had again torn open. Jack was sick with remorse. He tried again to decide where he might head the fox, and raced toward the head of a little draw. No longer did he want to shoot a fox, but only to catch his beloved dog. Thunder's paws must hurt, but Thunder had all the fighting heart of a fine hound. He would run until he could run no more.

The fox did not come up the draw and it was three hours later before Jack caught Thunder. Leaving the sore-footed hound behind, the fox had long since disappeared. Jack heard Thunder coming and waited for him. Leaning his shotgun against a tree, he flung himself on the laboring puppy and bore him to the snow. Thunder wriggled in protest, for he knew the trail hadn't ended. But Jack held him until he quieted, and snapped the chain back on his collar.

Thunder's paws were so badly torn that it was doubtful if he could run again all winter long.

Chapter 5   Outlaw

Star lay under a flowering azalea, luxuriating in the warmth of the spring sun. At long last the winter lay behind.

It had been a violent time, a season of heavy snows, high winds, and searing cold. The ground had not been bare since the first snow fell, and there had been very few thaws. Only the strong, the wise, and the lucky had seen the snows finally melt and fill the rivers and creeks and roilly ponds. There was no nook or corner of the wilderness that had not witnessed or did not conceal a tragedy. Star knew of one yard where only three of twenty-seven deer had survived.

Though he'd had his hungry days, Star had fared
better than most. He was young, strong, and, as
winter had tightened its harsh grip over the wilderness, he had acquired wisdom. Above all, he had
discovered that it paid to haunt the deer yards.
Sooner or later an exhausted or starved animal was
sure to fall, and during the early part of the winter
there had always been a battle over the carcass.
Coyotes, other foxes, weasels, mink, fisher, carniv-
orous birds, and even mice and snowshoe rabbits
had competed for the bounty. As the season advanced there were so many dead deer that competition was not so fierce, and on the whole meat-eaters
had done reasonably well.

During the winter Star had learned much more
than just how to survive.

Though Dade Matson was not liked for himself,
everybody in the valley respected his woodcraft and
hunting ability. And Dade's tale of a Haunt Fox
with an extra toe on each front paw was accepted
without question. There were nine hounds in the
valley, plus an assortment of mongrels supposed to
be hunting dogs. The master of every dog was eager
to prove his dog's worth and his own hunting
prowess by bringing in the Haunt Fox, and every
dog in the valley, or so the owner said, had been on
Star's trail at least once. The fact that nobody had
been able to kill him served only to heighten the
reputation that had attached itself to him. Star was

famous all out of proportion to anything he had
managed to do so far.

Actually he had been run by hounds only five
times, and of all that had run him, only one had
pressed him really hard. That was a long-legged,
fast-driving hound owned by Eli Catman, who had a
farm at the head of the valley. Eli had had the only
sight of or shot at Star, but he had shot at such a
hopeless distance that the pellets merely stung.
However, Eli had thought him much nearer than he
really was and so he had reported. He thought he
should have killed him, and thus, in addition to his
other accomplishments, it was believed that the
Haunt Fox bore a charmed life.

Throughout, Star had learned. His was the vitality and bursting life of a young creature that is in
perfect physical condition. He liked to play, and he
loved to have a hound on his trail because that was
the most delightful of sports. Now he had learned
that men usually accompanied the hounds and Eli's
stinging shot had proven to him that they could be
very dangerous. But he had also altered his concep-
tion of humans.

Before he had merely feared and evaded them.
He had discovered, while running ahead of their
hounds, that men in the woods are blundering and
helpless. A fox that ran into the wind could always
smell them in time to get out of harm's way. If,
because of circumstances, a fox had to run with the

wind, he could avoid men simply by choosing his
course. Men never penetrated briar or laurel thickets. They hesitated to go into groves of small hemlocks, where lower branches brushed the ground.
They didn't like to go among tangled masses of boulders. Almost always, when waiting for their hounds,
they chose a spot where trees were widely spread.
Star had learned to anticipate in advance about
where he would find a hunter standing and had also
taught himself tricks which few foxes, wise as they
are, ever learn. Instead of circling in conventional
fashion when pursued, he would sometimes choose
to run straight away.

Without question he accepted the fact that all
men were his enemies and that he could expect
quarter from none, and that influenced his attitudes
toward them. He did not hate them, as he did his
mortal enemy, Stub, but in his devious way he recognized the challenge made by men and dogs.

He lay quietly beneath the azalea, burrowed
deep into the cool earth, and watched everything
about him. Not twenty feet away a mother blue jay
nested in a stunted sassafras bush; Star could see
her tail feathers thrust over the rest of the nest. He
had little interest in her, except for watching, because he had fed well early in the morning and he
was not hungry. However, he had marked the nest
against future need. Soon it would be crowded with

nestlings and it was near enough to the ground so that a leaping fox might easily knock it down.

Only Star's eyes moved as a silent flying grouse whirred into a copse of evergreens. He rose, mouth parted slightly and tongue lolling. Although he was not hungry, grouse were a delicacy that he would accept any time. Star arched his neck and tilted his head slightly as he sought the grouse's scent.

The blue jay saw him. Ordinarily she would have been screaming from the safety of some tree, but now she merely hugged her nest a little tighter and did not move. She had a nest to protect and any noise on her part was sure to center attention on it.

Ears erect, face alert, and gorgeous tail curled behind him, Star padded on black paws toward the covert in which he had seen the grouse come down. He moved slowly, rippling along rather than trotting or walking, and only a very observant eye would have seen him at all. He circled slightly to get into the wind.

Full in the shifting breezes he stood still, one front paw curled beneath him and pointed nose questing. A buck deer had passed through the evergreens within the past two hours, and his scent remained strong. Mice crawled in their earth-bound lairs beneath the needle-carpeted floor, and a jerky-tailed chipmunk squeaked on a moss-grown stump. But there was no scent of grouse and Star was puzzled. He had seen the grouse go into the thicket but certainly it was not there now. At any rate, he couldn't smell it.

Star could not know that he wasn't supposed to smell it. The winter had taken a heavy toll of wilderness life and spring was the time for rebuilding. There was hardly a copse or thicket that some mother or mother-to-be had not already claimed for herself or was not examining with a furtive eye, and nature had readied the wilderness creatures for raising young. Though she had a pronounced odor all the rest of the year, in this time of motherhood when she must necessarily be limited to a small area surrounding her nest, the nesting grouse had no scent. Star passed within five feet of her and did not even suspect she was there.

Finally tiring of the search, he wandered to the other end of the thicket and passed through. Trotting slowly up a ridge, Star whirled suddenly and streaked at top speed back in the direction from which he had come.

He had caught the odor of Soft Foot, a big dog fox whose mate nursed a brood of young in an underground den. Always restless and always ranging, hard put to feed his mate and cubs, Soft Foot permitted no other fox to intrude on the hunting range he had chosen for himself. He crossed Star's trail and pursued him across a wooded ridge into a rocky valley, and stopped when Star passed beyond the boundaries that Soft Foot had decided he could defend.

For the second time in an hour Star passed a new baby of the woods without even knowing it was there. Venturing through a stand of young aspens in which tangled rhododendron grew, he all but stepped on a spotted fawn that lay outstretched on the ground. Never so much as twitching an ear, the fawn blended so perfectly with its surroundings that not even a hawk could have seen it. Like the nesting grouse, it had no scent.

Star put speed in his lagging paws when he heard a wrathful snort and the sound of thudding hoofs. The fawn's mother, a little three-year-old doe with her first baby, had always been ready to flee from anything at all. Now, with a helpless fawn depending on her, she had all the courage of an aroused lion. The doe was ready to give instant battle to anything that ventured into her nursery, and to use all her wiles and cunning to keep her fawn from harm. She chased Star what she considered a safe distance away and returned to her baby.

Star halted, wondering. Of the wilderness himself, he could not hope to survive unless he knew the habits of other wilderness creatures. He thought he had known them. However, never before had he witnessed anything like this and his curiosity was aroused. For a moment after the doe stopped chasing him he sat on a ledge, tail curled about his legs and face keen with interest. Then he slunk back toward the thicket.

Choosing his route carefully, he stayed in a whispering little breeze that eddied out of the thicket and kept him informed of the doe's whereabouts. Nervous because Star had been there, she was lingering near the fawn. Star, like most wild things, knew how to be patient, and stayed where he was. He could not see the doe, but he quested for scents with his nose and kept his pointed ears erect. There was mystery here, something he did not understand, and he must not leave until he did.

Presently the doe went away to forage and Star crept forward. He hadn't the faintest notion of what he was looking for, but there was another and more experienced woods prowler who did know why does haunted thickets at this time of the year. Stub, the renegade, had also seen the doe, and was creeping forward on a course that paralleled that of the fox. Neither knew of the other because both were quiet as ghosts and their scents did not cross.

Star walked slowly, not crouching because he wanted to see as much as possible. He stopped at a tiny fluttering of wings, but it was only a song sparrow that had alighted for an instant on a swaying aspen branch. The bird flew, and the branch moved slightly. Star continued his stealthy forward motion, veering a little to the left.

That move, entirely by chance, set both the fox

and the wild cat on courses that would converge within inches of the fawn. Stub was just a little ahead of Star, who, having the keener senses, became aware of the wild cat before Stub knew of his presence.

Star halted on a little sun-sprayed hillock where an eddying breeze had brought him knowledge of Stub. He crouched, melting down and then holding absolutely still. His tail was stiff, like an angry dog's, and he bristled slightly. He blended almost perfectly with red-gold sun shadows that flitted across the clearing.

Hatred surged within him. He had never forgotten his bosom comrade, Brush, nor the fact that Stub had killed his brother. Now his arch-enemy was before him. Star saw Stub come out of the laurel into a little opening.

The wild cat came like another shadow, visible against the forest's floor but moving so quietly and so stealthily that only the keenest eye would have seen him. Without seeming to move, Star arched his neck, and his yellow eyes burned as he kept them on Stub. The wild cat, who knew very well that there was a fawn nearby and that he had only to find it, was hunting by sight alone. Long since Stub had learned that fawns have no scent. But they were worth finding because they furnished a tender and tasty meal. With steady slowness he padded forward, darting his eyes wherever a fawn might be.

He looked toward the hillock upon which Star lay, and might have seen the fox except, at that moment, his eye was caught by the fawn's flicking ear.

The fawn was lying about thirty feet away, at the base of three aspens that grew very close together. Left there by the doe, ordinarily it would have lain perfectly still. However, the fawn had been discovered by a bar-winged fly with a vicious bite and a yearning for blood, and the fly had just bitten the fawn's ear. The fawn had flicked its ear in an effort to rid itself of the tormentor, and now Stub knew where it was.

The wild cat did not hurry. An aroused doe with a fawn to defend was fury itself and Stub wanted to find where the doe was, and whether or not she was near enough to attack, before he killed the fawn. On silent paws he padded forward until he was within six feet of Star. There he stopped, eyes still on the fawn, paws lightly planted, and head tilted. Star's seething nerves, stretched to an unendurable tension, suddenly exploded.

When he sprang, he knew exactly what he was doing. Though Stub needed only the split part of a second to realize that he was being attacked, Star was upon him, had slashed, and was away, before the cat could strike back. Blood dribbled down the wild cat's mottled, silky hide where Star's seeking jaws had found their target. Stub snarled and spat.

Almost the same motion that carried Star to his

enemy carried him out of harm's way. He whirled
against a tree, his face a savage fighting mask. When
Stub launched a charge that was intended to over-
whelm his attacker, Star was no longer there. When
Stub leaped, the fox dived in for another strike at
his enemy's flank, and was away two inches ahead of
Stub's raking claws.

There was a wrathful snort and a rattling of brush.
As the doe, attracted by the muted sounds of battle,
came angrily to her baby's defense, Star leaped behind a patch of laurel and continued to run. The
doe, fury incarnate, concentrated her anger on
Stub. She struck him with her front hoofs, rolling
him over twice, until Stub leaped up into an aspen.
For almost an hour the doe circled the tree, rearing
in attempts to reach the cat, and striking with her
hoofs until the trunk was fuzzy with shredded bark.
Finally she abandoned her vigil and led her baby to
another and safer thicket.

Meantime, Star had run only until he was sure
that he was not pursued, then settled down to a
steady trot. He had met and battled his enemy, but
the score remained unsettled because he had not
killed him. Star would not rest contented as long as
Stub roamed the wilderness. Hatred for the cat still
burned within him.

He hunted into a thicket where cottontails usually abounded, only to discover that Vixen had been
there before him. Vixen had not mated this season

either, and eagerly Star sniffed her tracks. At various times during the spring and winter they had hunted together and bedded together, but their trails hadn't crossed for some time and Star was happy to find sign of his friend. He discovered where she had caught and eaten a rabbit and for the moment remained undecided as to whether or not he should go find her. But he didn't because he was hungry. Before doing anything else he wanted to fill his belly, and the sort of hunting he intended to do now he preferred to do alone.

Downhill he swung, toward the valley and the farms. A rising excitement mounted within him, and a mischievous light danced in his eyes. He knew he was inviting trouble, but that sure knowledge served only to add seasoning to the venture he was about to undertake.

The sun had dipped, leaving the valley in shadow and painting the tops of the hills a pure, burnished gold when Star came to the edge of the woods and looked out at the few trees and straggling clumps of brush between him and the Crowley fields.

Behind his team of ponderous-footed work horses, Jeff Crowley was hurrying to guide a harrow over a newly plowed field so that it might be seeded tomorrow. Ambling slowly in from the pasture, the cows were snatching at last bits of green grass as they drifted toward the barn. In a pen by themselves, spring calves kicked up their heels. Chickens, ducks, geese, and turkeys, surfeited after a long day of eating, gathered in the barnyard and pecked idly at the food they found.

Star could neither see nor smell Jack or Thunder, though they were both there, Thunder sleeping in the sunshine and Jack working in the cow barn. Keeping in the shelter of an irregular line of small bushes, Star stalked toward a new-leafed maple tree.

He crouched near it, and once more looked the farm over. Star knew very well that Thunder lived here—not forgotten was that stormy night when Thunder had been on his trail. He did not fear the hound, for Star had since discovered that he could easily run away from most dogs.

Suddenly Star froze in his tracks.

Most of the Crowley poultry, knowing very well that night was upon them, were staying near the poultry house. But a little flock of speckled guinea fowl, half wild anyhow, were feeding near the maple. Finally, as though they were of one mind, they stopped catching the grasshoppers upon which they had been feeding, shook their wings, and ran like pheasants closer to the maple tree, where they intended to roost for the night.

Star did not move until they were close upon him. Then he sprang, snapped, and had a guinea fowl in his mouth before it knew what had happened. With a wild thrashing of wings the rest scattered and set up their unearthly screaming. His prize in his mouth, Star neither stopped nor looked back. But, in fleeing, he landed squarely on an ant hill and left his tracks plainly printed there. As he ran he heard Jeff Crowley shout. Star risked a fleeting glance to see Jeff, his team abandoned, running toward the tree.

Star ran fast only until he was in the woods. Then he sought a convenient thicket and stopped to feed. From time to time he interrupted his meal to arch his head toward his back trail. No hound bayed on it and there was no sign whatever of pursuit. Star finished the guinea fowl, licked his chops, and paced happily into the hills.

There was no pursuit because Jeff had a hunter's dislike of running a hound anywhere except on snow. Besides, Thunder was still just a puppy and night was at hand. No doubt he would take the fox's track, but letting him go on it meant to risk losing him in the forest. Jeff did find Star's paw prints in the ant hill, and recognized them. Only a bold and cunning animal would raid, while it was still daylight, so near a house. Star, the Haunt Fox, was now marked in more ways than one. Jeff studied the possibility of setting traps near the maple tree in the event that Star might make a return visit. He decided against it. The guinea fowl were fond of roosting in the tree and often the turkeys fed around it.

Instead of Star, traps might catch some of his own stock or someone's prowling dog.

Star, however, did not go back to the tree. He had caught one guinea fowl there and knew the rest might still be around. But he knew also that he had been noticed. It was not the part of wisdom to hunt too often in the same place. For two weeks Star kept strictly to the hills without going near the farms at all.

Even so, he added to his outlaw's reputation. Jeff Crowley told the story of the raid and it was passed along, with variations, from one end of the valley to the other. One night a raiding coyote got in Mike Tallant's sheep yard and left half a dozen lambs with their throats slashed. Nobody saw the raider come or go and nobody found any of his tracks. In spite of the fact that those who really knew foxes doubted if they killed in such a fashion, Star was given credit for this raid, too. A day later, in broad daylight, a fox leaped from the willows into a flock of ducks swimming in a creek and made off with the biggest and fattest. He was seen, and because the Haunt Fox was the center of attention, this raid was also blamed on him.

The valley rose against him. There was even some talk of an organized hunt to wipe out all foxes. Cooler and more knowing heads pointed out the folly of such ideas. Foxes were not sheep to be led to slaughter, but wise and cunning creatures. If everybody in the valley who could hold a club or gun joined the hunt, they still wouldn't get all the foxes. In the second place, this was the farmers' busiest season and if everyone went running off to hunt foxes, who would do the work? Neglecting their farms would do more damage than fox raids. It was far better, if Star was to be killed, to let some expert like Dade Matson handle the matter.

But before Dade could get on his trail, Star made another raid.

He was prowling near the head of the valley when a familiar odor drifted to his nostrils. It was just after nightfall, and Star stopped in his tracks while the scent of Eli Catman wafted to him. Star remembered last winter, when Eli's hard-running hound had been on his trail, and the shotgun pellets that had scorched his hide. Though of course he did not know the whys and wherefores of shotguns, Star had known perfectly well that Eli, in some mysterious manner, had the power to reach out and hurt from a long distance away.

That, however, had been in the daytime, and this was night. Star stood still, unafraid. He trotted a little way to get into stronger wind currents and smelled Eli's hound. Star ran his tongue out. He respected Eli's hound, but, increasingly sure of his own powers, he was confident that he could outrun any dog or throw it off the trail when he wearied of running. Star did a nervous little dance in the black night, for a new and interesting scent mingled with the odors blowing to his nostrils.

More than two years ago Eli had decided that there was money to be made in rabbit pelts, and he had bought a supply of breeding stock. Though they had been housed in hutches, the rabbits had overflowed their living space and now found shelter wherever they could around Eli's barn and outbuildings.

Star slunk forward to where a dozen or more of Eli's big rabbits were eating grass. He took one, and the rest were so little disturbed that they didn't even move. These were no wild cottontails or snowshoes, but tame things that had long since grown dull because they had for so long enjoyed man's protection. Star carried his prize back into the forest and ate until he could eat no more.

Ordinarily he wouldn't have gone back for a long time, but there had been no outcry and he suspected that he had not been discovered. The next night he visited Eli's again and took another rabbit. This was a rich discovery. Not only was it unnecessary to hunt these stupid rabbits, but there was as much meat in one as there was in four cottontails. For the next seven nights Star went back to Eli's and took one rabbit each night. He learned to enjoy only the choicest portions, leaving the rest for carrion hunters. Star even grew fat.

Eli, who had learned the hard way that raising rabbits is not the surest way to get rich quick, had fallen into the habit of paying little attention to his stock. So he noticed nothing wrong and did not bother to investigate until one morning when he failed to see a big, distinctively marked black and white rabbit that had always stayed near a shed. When Eli did look, he found Star's tracks.

A good woodsman, Eli discovered for himself that Star had been laying up by day in the nearby woods and raiding every night. Like Jeff, Eli hesitated to run a hound except on snow. However, he took his hound out on a leash and tracked Star to a thicket Star had used as a dining room. Rabbit fur and bones were all about.

Eli swore a mighty oath that one day the Haunt Fox would pay for these raids. Meantime, Star's fame grew.

Chapter 6 Heat Madness

Terror came on rays of a burning sun so hot that grasses shriveled and leaves wilted. Birds stalked about with mouths gaping and wings raised so that whatever breezes there were might touch them. Cattle grazed only in the cool of the early morning or late evening, and stood throughout the heat of the day in the shade of trees or belly-deep in water. Dogs burrowed close to the earth for whatever comfort might be found there. After the hardest winter anyone could remember the hottest and driest summer followed.

Rain seemed a thing of the past. Creeks that had been high over their banks in spring dwindled away

87

to a succession of shallow pools and lazy riffles from which boulders raised sun-scorched backs. Even when the sun finally dipped behind the western ridges, there were few refreshing breezes, though the nights at least afforded relief from the scorching sun. It was this setting that brought the madness.

Jack Crowley was the first to come in direct contact with it. Thunder tagging lazily at his heels, he was strolling up the road late one summer afternoon, when the hound suddenly crowded against his legs and whined uneasily.

Jack touched the dog and found him trembling. Never before had he known Thunder to fear anything. A little shiver traveled up Jack's spine.

"Come on, Thunder," he said, with a confidence that he did not feel.

Thunder stayed very close. He bristled, and an uneasy growl bubbled from his lips. Jack looked around for a club or rock and saw none close at hand. In the woods he might find a weapon, but suddenly he was afraid to go into the brush at all.

Just then the red fox appeared.

It came like a ghost into the scattered brush bordering the road. It was alive, but it had neither the aim nor the purpose of a living thing, and paid no attention whatever to obstacles in its path. It bumped into a dead stick that leaned at an angle against a tree, pushed stupidly against it, and advanced only when the stick accidentally fell.

Jack stared, horrified. Foxes were vital things, alive from the tips of their black noses to the last hair on their furred tails. They were far too cunning even to show themselves to a human, to say nothing of blundering along within a few feet of one.

Thunder, who had been born to hunt foxes, whimpered in fear and slunk close to Jack's side.

The beast came nearer, descending a little slope and half falling into the road. The eyes that it turned on Jack and Thunder seemed to see nothing, but a red glare burned within them. At a slow and purposeful walk, the fox came toward them, lips curled back from polished fangs. Then it paused, distracted by the whispering of the little stream that paralleled the road. For a full ten seconds it studied the water, then stumbled toward it.

Jack found his legs. Thunder at his heels, he raced up the road toward the farmhouse. Sweat streaked his forehead, fear made his heart beat faster. As he clattered up the steps of the back porch, his father opened the door.

"What's the matter, Bub?"

"The fox!" Jack gasped.

"Take it easy," Jeff counseled. "Cool off, and tell me what happened."

Jack gained control of himself and told the story. Jeff listened intently, then asked leading questions. Had the fox really come that close to a human being intentionally, or had Jack surprised it? Exactly how had it looked and acted? Did Jack think it was sick?

When the story was finished, Jeff looked grave. Every now and again there was an outbreak of rabies among wild foxes, and it was always serious. A mad fox lost all its usual caution and shyness. It would go anywhere, attack anything, and its bite was as deadly as a puff adder's. Jeff took his shotgun from its rack, filled the magazine with shells, and pumped one into the chamber.

"Let's go have a look at your fox."

Jack's mother looked worriedly at them. "Be careful."

"Don't you worry," Jeff reassured her. "We'll be all right."

Thunder trailed them a little ways from the porch, stopped, curved his tail against his haunches, and trotted back to the porch. The hound wanted no part of this terror. He sat on the porch and stared with solemn eyes as Jack and Jeff walked down the road.

They came to the thicket, looked down at the creek, and saw the fox threading its way among exposed boulders. It stopped to launch a senseless attack on one of the boulders, and Jeff raised his shotgun. Turning, the fox saw them. It came suddenly alive, made a great leap that carried it over the stones, and charged straight at the pair. Jeff held his fire until the beast was within ten yards, then shot. A little cloud of dust burst from its fur as the pellets found their mark. The fox tumbled end over end and lay still.

Jeff pumped another shell into the chamber and shot again. Already dead, the fox was flung an inch or two backward as this second charge of shot pounded into it. Nevertheless, Jeff readied his shotgun once more before moving forward.

They looked down at the dead creature. Except that it was literally crawling with fleas, which no healthy fox would tolerate, in death there was nothing to mark it from any normal beast. Thoughtfully Jeff prodded it with his foot.

"We could tell positively after a laboratory examination," he said, "but there's not much point because I'm sure it's rabies. I'll call Doc Wittmeyer out to inoculate the dogs, and we'd better watch the stock. Until this thing's run its course, have a shotgun or a good strong club in easy reaching distance no matter where you go—even out to the barn."

"How long will it be?"

"I can't even guess," Jeff said. "It may be just a light attack and it may be an epidemic that will run a long while." He looked sadly at the dead beast. "There won't be as many foxes on the snow next winter."

Jack said, "Look!"

There was a small meadow across the creek, and

at the far end of it another fox appeared for a fleeting instant and disappeared in the brush. Jeff watched it slip out of sight.

"Well, not all of them have it. That big one has certainly escaped so far."

Jack said impulsively, "I hope the Haunt Fox comes through!"

"Why?"

Jack stopped, embarrassed. He had had great dreams of running foxes on snow. He had found only failure; Thunder hadn't been able to run at all after his second hunt. But Jack still thought secretly of the Haunt Fox. Thunder would run him again some time, and who brought the Haunt Fox in would be supreme among fox hunters. Jack had already made up his mind that, if there was any possible way to do it, he would be that hunter.

Jeff flashed one of his rare and understanding smiles. "I hope he makes it all right, too," he said. "Well, I'll get a shovel and bury this one. Poor devil. Shooting's the best thing that could have happened to him."

Across the creek, Star stopped as soon as he was safely hidden in the brush. He had come down from the hills for the express purpose of making another raid on the Crowley farm, and had stopped when he caught scent of the rabid fox that, when Star approached, was stumbling aimlessly among the boulders. For a few minutes Star watched, and saw Jeff and Jack return with the shotgun.

Star was not at all worried about the men, but he was troubled by the nearness of the rabid fox. Like the hound, without knowing exactly what it was, he knew that something was terribly wrong. He had seen other rabid foxes, and was more afraid of them than he had ever been of anything else.

He heard the shotgun blast. The sound made him nervous, but he did not run because he knew that he had not been seen. Taking advantage of the cover afforded by boulders and brush, Star slunk toward the deeper woods. Trotting across the little meadow, he suspected that the watching men saw him. But he did not worry about it. The covering forest was only a short way ahead and he was soon in it.

For the past weeks Star had lived alone. He had not run across Vixen's trail and did not know that Vixen, feeling the urge to roam, had gone to the other side of the watershed where Star made his home. Even if Vixen had been present, Star would not have traveled with her. Here, in this infected region, he feared everything except himself.

Star trotted easily up a timbered ridge and into a blackberry patch at the summit. He halted, sat down, and scratched the right side of his neck with his right hind paw. He turned to bite an itchy place

on his flank, then another on his side. Rabid foxes
no longer cared about fleas, but Star was not ill and
he liked to keep himself clean. Fleas bothered him.

He threaded his way through the blackberry
canes to an aspen forest that was studded with huge
boulders. A little stream, spring-fed and therefore
always cold, purled among the rocks. Star drank,
daintily balancing himself on a boulder, then followed the rill upstream.

For the most part, the stream consisted of swift
little riffles that gurgled among the boulders, but
there were a few pools wherein brook trout pursued
bugs that floated on the water. Though complete
darkness had not yet brought relief to a sweltering
wilderness, both sides of the little creek were cool.
A fat old woodchuck, resting in the shade, waddled
unwillingly aside when Star approached. The woodchuck clicked his teeth in protest. He paused at the
mouth of a crevice, ready to dive in if the fox
swerved toward him.

Star kept on going. He was hungry, but big wood-
chucks could put up a terrific battle and he had no
wish to fight for his dinner right now. Besides, he
was on a different mission. Star came to the end of
the scattered boulders and went on into a little
grove of aspens.

This was near the head of the valley, and the hills
on both sides were mere ridges. Here, among the

aspens, beaver had thrown a dam across the little creek. Over the years, as the beaver colony increased, the dam had grown so that now it reached halfway across the shallow valley. There were many little feeder dams, and up the creek some smaller beaver colonies.

A big beaver, swimming on top of the main pond, merely circled away as Star approached and did not sound an alarm by slapping the water with its tail. Beaver and foxes never had been enemies; neither had any wish to hurt the other.

Paying no attention to the beaver, Star pawed among the litter cast up at the side of the dam. As though he were about to play with it, he picked up an aspen stick from which beaver had chewed the bark. After a moment he cast the stick aside and chose another. The stick in his jaws, Star stepped quietly into the water.

He waded out, feeling his way in the mud bottom, and when he was beyond wading depth he swam. Star let himself sink, so that only the tip of his slim black muzzle showed above the water. The stick, clenched in his jaws, he did not allow to sink or become wet.

Behind him, his soaking-wet tail curled like a great fish hook, and in the cold water every hair stood straight. Star swam to the middle of the pond, turned in a looping curve, and swam back to where he could touch the mud bottom with his paws. For a moment he stood there, still almost submerged, then swam back into the pond again.

He stayed for a full twenty minutes in the water. When he finally struck for shore he left the stick floating on the pond. Star had accomplished his purpose. With no other dry place to go, the fleas had sought refuge on the stick. Star was clean again. He climbed out on the bank and in the waning daylight shook himself vigorously. Then he sat down and licked each of his paws.

There were four beaver on the bank now, each busily felling an aspen tree. This was summer, but the residents of the beaver colony knew that winter would come again. Their ponds would be frozen over, and they would be imprisoned beneath the ice. Summer was their working time and before another winter struck, the pond must contain enough food to see them through the cold season. Hard at work, the beaver paid no attention to the red fox as he trotted quietly past.

Star hesitated, uncertain as to whether he should hunt in the forest or go back to the Crowley farm and find something there. But he was a long way from the Crowleys now and the fine taste of adventure that raiding farms offered him had gone flat. Memory of the rabid fox was not a pleasant one. Star hunted in a hemlock thicket, found a covey of spring-born grouse that had not yet learned that it is wise to roost in trees, and caught and ate one.

He slept in the same thicket while the scattered covey, the survivors of which had flown blindly into the darkness, huddled wherever chance had brought them down. Star awakened often, and four times during the night he changed his position. The time of restful sleep and careless play had gone when the madness came.

In the next morning's dawn hours, Star left the thicket to trot back to the beaver dam. He drank while morning mists swirled from the pond. Then he shrank back, trying to hide in the mists and making no move that might betray his presence.

Down the ridge on the opposite side of the pond came a big male skunk. Like the rabid fox, the skunk was bereft of that vital spark which had made it alive and given it a character of its own. The madness had seized it. It mounted a felled tree and for a moment stood turning its short-necked head this way and that. Then it charged straight at a still-working beaver that had not yet become aware of its presence.

The beaver discovered the skunk in time, and tumbled at once into the pond. It halted long enough to slap the water with its tail, as a warning to the rest, then hastily submerged.

Without any hesitation the rabid skunk tumbled

after it. When its water-sleek head broke the surface, the skunk struck straight across the pond. It
had neither aim nor destination, and when it came
to a floating stick, the skunk tried to climb it. The
stick dipped beneath the surface, then bobbed up
again. Twenty times the skunk tried to climb upon
the stick. Its useless efforts grew weaker, and when
the stick finally floated away, the skunk swam feebly
after it. Skunk and stick went over the spillway, into
a smaller pool, and down that into a snarling riffle.

Star slunk quietly away. He had learned to match
his wits against everything that beset him, but wit
and cunning could not prevail against this terror. It
was everywhere and there was no way to avoid it.
Star jumped convulsively when a wild turkey hen
and its brood of young scattered before him. He
made no attempt to pursue them. Though he
wanted food, he was much more nervous than
hungry.

The sun rose, a burning ball in the sky, and Star
began to pant. He circled back toward the little
stream because he remembered that it was cooler
there. Reaching the stream, he sought a pool,
lapped up some cold water, and then lay in the
pool. Rising, he shook himself and walked up the
stream bed.

As he came nearer the source, the little stream
dwindled in size. There were dry stretches, where
such water as flowed had sought subterranean chan-

nels, and a few shrinking pools. These were filled with trout that had come from both up and down-stream, and Star nosed hopefully around some of the pools. However, though they contained a great many fish, all the pools were too deep for him to catch anything.

Other fish-eaters were doing well. A chattering kingfisher flew over Star's head, dive-bombed a pool a hundred yards upstream, and rose with a three-inch trout in its claws. A swimming mink's head broke water; it, too, had a fish. Star raced forward, intending to pirate the booty, but the mink slipped into a small crevice and snarled defiance. Star was almost at the head of the stream before he found anything to eat.

He came to a long and wide pool, so shallow that the back fins of some of the fish in it broke water even in the deepest part. Star waded in, and the school of trout surged frantically around him. The fox had only to dip his head and snap as they passed, and caught a fish every time. They were not large, but enough of them satisfied Star's appetite.

He trotted on to where the stream had its birth in a moss-grown spring that seeped from beneath a bank, and lapped a few mouthfuls of water. Then he started up over a rocky ridge, intending to cross the ridge and go down into the valley on its opposite side. Star knew of several cool places where he could lay up while the day's heat was at its worst.

Halfway across the ridge he whirled, and without stopping streaked as fast as he could in the opposite direction. Just in time had he caught the flash of motion within twenty feet of him.

It was Soft Foot, the dog fox who had hunted so faithfully for his mate and cubs. Soft Foot had felt the madness coming upon him and had deliberately turned his back upon his family, traveling as fast and as far as he could.

He had long since forgotten them, and everything else save the fever that burned his brain. Because he did not care to eat, he was gaunt. Fleas infested his body, but he did not care about them, either. He was tortured, and wanted to inflict his own torture upon whatever crossed his path. Having scented Star, Soft Foot had concealed himself and waited until Star was almost upon him before launching an attack. Now Soft Foot's speed and fury were those of a mad thing.

But Star's flight was born of desperation. A terrible fear gripped him; the knowledge that he must not let Soft Foot catch him was a raking spur that called for all the strength in his body and all the speed in his legs. He dared not risk a backward glance to see how near Soft Foot was. He must do nothing except run.

He flashed up a trail that wandering deer had worn deep, bounded high over a log, and felt something snap at his paw. Because he had thought for nothing else, he assumed it was Soft Foot's snapping jaws and summoned every last bit of speed that his wonderful legs could furnish.

Star ran another mile before feeling sure that he was no longer pursued. He slowed to a trot, his heart pounding and tongue lolling from spread jaws. Finally he stopped, forequarters raised on a rock while he examined his back trail. Nothing followed him.

Soft Foot was a mile back, twisted in one of Dade Matson's traps at the log where Star thought Soft Foot had snapped at him. Star himself had escaped one of the two traps by a hair's breadth; he had sprung it with his paw when he leaped over the log. Soft Foot had landed squarely in the second trap of the set.

Aroused by fear of the mad foxes, the farmers of the valley had offered a ten-dollar bounty for each rabid animal that was brought in, and Dade Matson was working hard. It was perhaps the kindest thing he had ever done, for the stricken beasts were doomed to wander in misery, and then most of them would die anyhow.

Star trotted on, cold fear still in his heart. All day he did not stop, and when night came he halted only long enough to hunt and eat. Then he traveled all night.

Dawn of the next day found him far back in the hills, miles from any place he had ever known before. He had had no thought save that he must not stay in his native range any longer. Now he found peace, for the disease had not reached this remote fastness.

All day long Star rested in a thicket. With night he went forth to hunt again, and stopped as the scent of another fox—a healthy one—crossed his nostrils.

Star raced happily forward to sniff noses with Vixen.

Chapter 7   The Vixen

When the summer heat waned so did the madness, and by the time the first frost glittered on yellow aspen leaves the wilderness was clean again.

It was also sadly ravaged. Few were the valleys and draws that lacked a pathetic heap of small whitened bones where kind death had finally over-taken a rabid animal. This year, except for spring cubs which had been affected hardly at all, there would not be many foxes to leave tracks in the new snow.

But those that were left found rich living. Because there were fewer foxes to help keep their numbers in control, cottontails, snowshoes, and mice swarmed in vast abundance. They gnawed the bark from trees and chewed the roots. Seeds falling from wild grasses were devoured almost as soon as they fell.

Rabbits and mice were not alone in competing for food. Prowling bears, sensing the winter to come and anxious to line their bellies with enough fat to see them through their long sleep, reared on ponderous haunches and pulled down branches of wild apple trees for the gnarled apples they bore. Or they climbed the trees, and by their weight alone dragged fruit-laden branches to the ground and left them dangling and broken.

Deer came too, eager for the luscious morsels. Antlered bucks, that had already left the bark of saplings hanging in shreds as they scraped velvet from growing antlers, nosed about for the delicacies. Trim does and spring-born fawns waited nervously near the edges of the groves, always alert to dash in and snatch fruit before a stronger and more vigorous buck could chase them away.

Competition for the better things that offered frequently led to fights. Star watched one such battle as he sat on a stone-studded hillside with his thick-furred tail curled around his rear paws. His belly was full, for his own hunting had been easy. Star tapped the earth with his front paws and curiously watched the scene unfolding below him.

There were five wild apple trees growing near the

bed of a swift-moving little mountain stream. The hot summer had given them an almost tropical fertility, for they had had an abundance of water to swell their roots and carry into them all the richness of the earth. The five apple trees had been full-laden, but were now nearly stripped by visits of hungry bears.

On the far side of the trees stood two does with spring-born fawns at their heels. The fawns lingered shyly behind their mothers while the does paced back and forth and watched a craggy-antlered buck rear to reach the apples that remained. There was motion in a neighboring thicket, and another buck came out of the forest. He was a little bigger than the one already at the apple trees, with massive and high-spreading antlers.

For a moment the two bucks faced each other belligerently, and shook their antlers at each other. But they were evenly matched and knew it, and they knew also that a fight would be a long affair. With succulent plunder to crop, and the does waiting, the bucks could afford to settle their differences at another time.

Star ran his tongue out and stretched his jaws in a prodigious yawn. Well-fed, he regarded with detached interest a big snowshoe hare that hopped down toward the apple trees and looked hopefully on. The snowshoe scurried back to hiding when one of the bucks made a short, savage dash at it.

A sudden gust of wind sent ripened apples pattering to earth and the bucks ate busily while the two does with their fawns rushed forward to seize what they could. With agile dashes and quick little leaps they evaded the bucks' lunging antlers.

Star turned his head as a little bear padded down the slope to take his share of the spoil. For a moment the bear and the biggest buck glared angrily at each other, then both fell to eating on opposite sides of the trees.

Then, as the fallen apples were eaten, the bucks lunged more savagely at the does and fawns and the bear swiped at them with his front paw. The bigger buck butted the smaller one's flank with his antlers, and in turn received a raking along his ribs. They snorted and jumped apart, lowering their heads and stamping their front hoofs as they took battle positions.

Star turned his head to sniff the breeze. Vixen, with whom he had run for a share of the time ever since he'd found her again, came down the hill to join him. They touched noses and she curled up beside him, as interested as he was in watching the byplay beneath the apple trees.

Lunging together, the two bucks met head on. Antler scraped antler, and seemed to generate a signal that sent red anger leaping in the eyes of both. They parted, and came together with a crashing of antlers. For a while they strained and pushed, the big muscles in their necks showing plainly as each strove to drive the other back.

Again they drew apart, and leaped together with a rattling of antlers that stirred echoes in the forest. The smaller buck made a quick pass at the bigger one's soft underbelly and missed. For a few minutes they sparred. Then they began slashing viciously with antlers and sharp front hoofs.

Suddenly the does and fawns, white tails over their backs, leaped into the forest and disappeared. Noiselessly as a puff of smoke, Vixen drifted softly up the hill and a moment later the bear took hasty flight.

Star, too, got the scent of Dade Matson, but for the time being he did not move. Long since he had learned to judge men, and Dade was still a good safe distance away. Star was too interested in the fighting bucks to leave before it was necessary.

After a moment he rose, his pointed nose in the wind. Dade was coming nearer. Star shuffled his front paws nervously. In a gap between the trees he saw Dade, and slipped quietly into a covert. Star lay behind a fallen tree, only his pointed ears and his eyes showing over it as he watched the trapper come on. He was hidden and he knew it.

Fighting furiously, with no time to look at anything else, the battling bucks continued to lunge and charge while Dade walked into the small clearing where the apple trees grew. He halted to watch the fight, and Star kept his eyes on him.

The bucks broke again. Breathing heavily, they glared at each other. Then a little breeze carried the scent of the silent watcher to them. They arched their necks and turned their heads, still on fire with the hot surge of battle. The bigger one walked stiff-leggedly toward Dade. He pawed the earth like an angry bull and shook his formidable crest of antlers.

Star's eyes brightened and he held very still. He knew a lot about men and their ways, but he did not understand much about their weapons. He saw Dade's hand slip to a holster as the trapper drew a revolver.

There was a thunderous explosion. The big buck trembled, took three staggering forward steps, and turned to leap away. But his supple muscles no longer obeyed. The slug from Dade's revolver had gone deep, and the buck's leap was broken as soon as he started it. He pitched forward on his nose, made a valiant effort to get up, and collapsed. The smaller buck raced for the safety of the woods.

Star glided away, afraid of Dade Matson and the terrible forces at Dade's command, but not so frightened that he would betray his presence by a hasty or ill-considered move. Like a stalking cat he inched close to the ground, keeping the log between himself and Dade until he reached a big boulder and then using that as a shield. Finally he rounded a copse of brush and looked carefully back toward the apple trees.

He could still hear and smell Dade as the trapper dressed the fallen buck, but he could not see him and was reasonably certain that Dade could not see either. Star rose and raced up the hill until he thought he was safe, then subsided to a trot. While the sun was at its highest he slept in the shade of some cool evergreens.

Lately there had developed within him a restless longing. This was not his native range, the country in which he had been born, and he missed the old familiar trails that his paws had trod since earliest puppyhood. Here he had come because he feared the summer madness and here he might come again should there ever be a good reason for it. But it was not his true home, and, now that the summer madness was gone, he could go back to the range he liked best.

In addition, there were strange impulses and urges arising within him. The thought of Vixen, who, until this time had been only a playmate and hunting companion, was strangely troubling. With nightfall, Star set off deliberately to find her and discovered her hunting in a thicket.

Always before Star had sought Vixen only when he was lonely, but now that he was back with her again he felt a strange sense of contentment and fulfillment. Star was older, more mature, and though the mating moon had not yet come, this was the year that he would take a mate. What he felt were the first powerful stirrings that would result in such an important step.

Slowly, sometimes separated but never very far apart, they worked back to the hills rising above the Crowley farm. Star saw Soft Foot's forlorn mate, who flashed ivory fangs in the autumn moonlight. Hers had been a desperate struggle. After Soft Foot left she had had to provide food for and protection for a brood of five cubs. Now the cubs had gone their own way and her burden was eased, but Soft Foot's memory lingered painfully with her. Not until that memory faded would she be ready to mate again. At present she wanted no dog foxes with or even near her.

Star made no attempt to approach her, but when he saw one of Soft Foot's sons, one of two cubs that had escaped Dade Matson, he chased it. Star was a male fox, approaching the mating season. Any other male of his own species must necessarily pose a threat. However, he did not chase the cub very far. If they met next year they might battle, but now the cub was too small to be a real danger.

Hunting when they were hungry, sleeping where they became tired and sometimes even back-tracking a little, they worked slowly back toward Star's beloved home range. On a night when a full autumn moon rode so low in the heavens that it seemed to be rolling right on top of the silhouetted hills, they stood within a few feet of the hillside den where Star had been born.

It was an earthen den, an old woodchuck hole which had been enlarged by Star's father and mother. The woodchuck, the den's first occupant, had selected his home with a view to utilizing all natural advantages. It was situated squarely in the center of a patch of little evergreens whose lower branches brushed the ground. There was a big boulder in the center of the thicket, and the woodchuck had excavated his home beneath that. It was a snug den, one which was never dampened by melting snow water or ground seepage. And it was well hidden.

Star trotted over to his old home. No trace remained of the warm and full life that had been there. Rain, snow and wind had worked their will with the place, obliterating all scent. Leaves had blown into the den's entrance. Star sniffed about and walked over to sit beside Vixen.

The bright moon rose higher, flooding the valley with a soft and mellow light that left deep shadow in some places and revealed others almost as clearly as if it had been day. The trees on the ridges, silhouetted against the moon, stirred softly. Frost-withered grasses rippled in the wind.

Star felt a mighty surge of life within him. He

circled Vixen in a gallant little dance, then halted in his tracks.

From the opposite ridge came the musical, full-throated call of another male fox. Star bristled. But Vixen was on her feet, standing rigidly, giving eager attention to the sound and to the ridge from which it came. Her eyes gleamed, her jaws parted, and her tongue lolled slightly as she listened for a repetition of the enticing call.

Star felt a fierce surge of blind rage. He turned, snarled at his companion, and then faced the ridge from which the other fox had called. Again the yearning plea rolled forth, and Star snarled again. Curling his bushy tail around his legs, he pointed his slim muzzle at the sky and answered. Thus he served notice that he was here and here he intended to stay. Whoever and whatever took away what was his must fight for it.

Down in the valley, ears for which they had never been intended also caught the sounds of the night-calling foxes. Eli Catman, journeying to his home at the head of the valley, had stopped to call on the Crowleys, and was taking his leave. Jack and Jeff had followed him out on the porch, and Thunder walked to the edge of the porch and stood with his fine muzzle upraised in the stirring breeze. The two men and the boy stood still, spellbound by the feeling that has fascinated hunters since the first man and the first hound hunted together. Thunder whined softly, and held his body tense. None of the men spoke or even moved until the last rippling echoes of the challenge had died away in the forest. Then Eli Catman turned to Jeff Crowley, a pleased smile on his face.

"Seems like there's still some left," he said. Suddenly he was seized with inspiration. "Let's have a fox chase!"

"A good idea!" Jeff agreed. "The moon's just right!"

"I'll bring my hound!" Eli said eagerly. "Jack, you bring Thunder. We'll get Dade Matson to fetch his two, and Tom Parker and George Sedlack. We'd ought to round up a decent pack. How about tomorrow night?"

"Swell!" Jeff dropped a big hand on Jack's shoulder. "That suit you, Bub?"

Thus, at moonrise the next night, Star was startled in the thicket where he was hunting rabbits by the sudden and unexpected baying of a hound. Star stopped in his tracks, recognizing Thunder's voice. A moment later Eli Catman's hound blended his voice with Thunder's, then George Sedlack's dog. The rest of the pack of nine chimed in as they caught the scent. Some bayed at sporadic intervals, but only Eli Catman's hound and Thunder tongued steadily.

Star danced nervously, for this was one of the things that he remembered well. He licked his chops with a delicate tongue and turned to sniff the wind. Eagerly he reared up, with his black front paws on a stump, looking in the direction where the tonguing pack ran. A great excitement rippled through him.

Star walked a little distance, then ran three hundred yards to the summit of a stone-studded hill. He sat down, tail curled around his rear paws and neck arched as he looked back toward the baying hounds. A moment later he knew they were on his trail.

Star streaked away, trying no ruses now because the full freshness of an abundant life swelled strongly within him. He could outrun the pack, he knew it, and he wanted to run. Star heard their voices fading in the moonlit night; already they were strung out with the slower dogs trailing far behind. Thunder and Eli Catman's hound bayed strongly in the lead.

Deliberately Star slowed his pace, luring the hounds on. He trotted slowly down the ridge to a small stream, waded into the water, and went up the stream for fifty yards. He walked out on the same side he had entered, shook himself dry, and raced back up the hill. Thunder and Eli Catman's hound came to the stream, coursed about, picked up the trail in twenty seconds, and swept strongly on.

These two powerful, fast hounds were far in advance of the rest now. Two hundred yards behind them ran one of Dade Matson's dogs, and four of the six remaining were still on the trail. One had not picked up the scent at all and another, running only a little way, had lazily gone back to the campfire where the men waited.

At the fire, a toasted sandwich in one hand and a glass of sweet cider in the other, Jack Crowley stood beside his father, listening to hound music that floated into the night and seemed to hang, without fading, in the air. Far in the distance, Thunder's bass roars and the more shrill yelps of Eli Catman's hound were faint but audible. It was easy to tell which dogs were leading. There was a quiet gleam of pride in Jack's eyes as he resumed his seat by the fire.

Nobody spoke, for speech would break the spell. Not even Dade Matson had a gun. All sat here solely because they loved to hear hounds run.

On a faraway ridge, still feeling the full surge of his youthful vitality. Star was merely playing with the dogs. Now and again, solely for the sake of making the hounds work it out, he left a break in his trail. He had nothing but contempt for all save the two leading hounds; they were the only ones that offered him anything like a genuine contest. Keeping as close as they could to their quarry, they never faltered for more than a moment or two at any trail break.

In a sudden burst of speed, Star raced up a ridge
and down into a valley on the other side. So far did
he lead the hounds that for almost an hour they
were out of hearing of the men around the campfire.
Then, deliberately, he swung back toward the waiting men. This was night, and Star knew very well
that men could not see him in the darkness.

Star passed within six hundred feet of the campfire, sniffed distastefully as swirling smoke stung his
nostrils, then ran to the top of the hill. He sat down,
tongue lolling and front paws nervous as he awaited
the hounds.

He had given an extra burst of speed to this run,
and now the hounds were far behind him. But they
came on, with Eli Catman's dog running fifty yards
behind Thunder. There was a shrill whistle from
Jack Crowley, and Thunder's tremendous roar became an uncertain yelp. Again he bayed, and again,
but when the whistle was repeated he went reluctantly into the campfire.

Then came the hoarse shout of Eli Catman, and
Eli's hound also left the trail and went in to his
master. Both hounds sat staring back into the moonlight. Both loved the trail and longed to run some
more, but they had learned to respect their masters'
commands. The other dogs, lacking the heart of
Thunder and Eli's hound, were glad enough to stop
running when they were summoned in.

The men at the fire had come out solely to hear a

fox chase and had had their fun. Now the hour was late and they must go home. They stamped out the fire and went their separate ways.

For twenty minutes after the men had gone, Star stayed where he was. As soon as he was positive the men were gone, he stalked down to the extinguished fire and circled it at a safe distance. The dead embers of the fire smelled rank in the night, as Star sniffed the scents of all the men. At one time or another he had crossed the trail of every man who had been there, and he knew them all. But they were all gone now, so Star padded to a spring to drink and then hunted in a thicket. He did not trouble to seek Vixen, but lay up by himself after he had eaten.

Lazy fall days faded into one another. Except for a few tough oaks and clusters of scrub beech where shriveled brown leaves would stay until spring, the hardwoods shed all their leaves and only the pines and hemlocks retained any foliage. The first snows came drifting gently to earth. Hunting became harder for many of the young spring- and summer-born wilderness creatures. But it was a far cry from last year's savage winter; the snows were not nearly as deep and game was more plentiful.

Running often with Vixen, but occasionally alone, Star played, hunted, and slept. There were a number of young foxes free-lancing happily through the wilderness in this, their first cold season and the only one that most of them would have without responsibilities. Next year those that survived would have mates and dens full of cubs. However, enough older animals had escaped the summer's scourge to provide breeding stock. Star knew of three mated pairs, and when he trespassed on their hunting grounds they invariably chased him. However, he had grown very big and strong. It was easy to run away and as yet he saw no special reason why he should stay and fight.

Dade Matson was often in the hills with his dogs these days, and sometimes other valley hunters. They took a great toll of the young and inexperienced foxes that had not yet learned how to run ahead of hounds or avoid hunters, but the foxes that escaped their first two or three runs quickly became wise.

Twice hounds were on Star's trail, but they were the inferior sort that he lost quickly. Now he had no desire to play with dogs and no time to waste on them, for the restless promptings and urges that had been so keen early in the fall were mounting unbearably.

As the winter advanced he never wanted to be far from Vixen. But Vixen seemed to take delight in avoiding him. When he was not hunting, he was seeking her.

One cold night when a new moon shone over the wilderness and outlined everything in soft relief, he found her hunting mice in a snow-covered meadow. Tufts of grass thrust frozen heads above the snow, and Vixen prodded among them with her nose. She reared, and came stiffly down with her front paws as she tried to pin a mouse between them.

Vixen paid absolutely no attention to Star when he walked out beside her. He sat down on the snow, tail straight behind him, head bent, ears pricked forward, eyes on Vixen. He made a pleading little noise in his throat. She ignored him.

Suddenly Star bristled. Over toward the edge of the meadow a shadow had appeared on the snow.

Vixen turned, sat down, and blinked her eyes solemnly. Into the meadow came another dog fox, the same that had flung his lonely lament to the skies last autumn. Arrogantly he trotted into the meadow, straight toward Vixen.

Snarling, Star glided forward to place himself between the challenger and Vixen. The other fox sat down on the snow, and a warning growl bubbled in his throat. Then, as though at a prearranged signal, they came together.

Vixen sat quietly, her tongue lolling slightly and eyes gleaming as she watched. She was the prize for which they fought and she knew it. What was more, she enjoyed it.

Star sidestepped a lunge at his slender front leg

and dodged in to slash at the other's neck. They reared, flailing at each other with their front paws as they sought a lethal hold. Star dropped suddenly to seize his enemy's right rear paw, and in turn felt slicing teeth cut through his fur into his flank.

Watching the gladiators thrust and parry, Vixen sat quietly, affecting complete disinterest in the battle's outcome. But an hour later, when the challenger ran three-legged back toward the forest out of which he had come, she lay like a small fur rug on the snow. Her rear paws were thrust back and her front ones forward, as Star, the winner, stood protectingly over her.

Never again, for as long as both lived, would he and Vixen be parted.

Chapter 8  Captive

Dade Matson was troubled and angry. All summer long, and into the autumn, he had trapped rabid foxes for the ten-dollar bounty offered. And, since nobody was inclined to take every dead fox to a laboratory, and determine whether or not it was infected with rabies, Dade had done quite well. But with midwinter his slack time arrived. Not only was the bounty withdrawn, but there were far fewer foxes.

Dade could still trap mink, muskrats, and raccoons along the stream beds, and do pretty well there as long as the weather remained mild. But with midwinter the streams were frozen, raccoons

121

were holed up, and muskrats swam beneath the ice. In cold weather, stream trapping was hard and often discouraging work.

There was a dollar bounty on weasels, but weasel pelts were worth little and it scarcely paid to lay a trap line for them alone. Always before in midwinter Dade had depended on foxes, and this year the regular bounty had been raised from two to four dollars. But there were far fewer of them. He ranged into the hills with his hounds, and for a while luck remained on his side. But the more stupid among the younger foxes soon fell before Dade's shotgun and the guns of others who also liked to hunt with hounds.

Dade resented the presence of other hunters. All of them had farms, jobs, or some other means of support. They were assured of a living. It did not seem to him that they should trespass in the woods and take what did not rightfully belong to them. Since he was the only one who took a full-time livelihood out of the woods, he thought he had first and strongest claim to whatever was there. The idea of sport alone, of hunting for the sheer joy of matching wits with some woods dweller, seldom entered his mind.

Finally he conceived what he thought was a marvelous plan.

There was a bounty on every fox caught, but the law did not specify how old that fox must be; even an hour-old cub would bring in the four dollars. As Dade well knew, wild vixens running the woods were due to have their cubs within a few weeks. However, to kill one of these now meant to collect the bounty on only one fox. By putting his plan in effect Dade could collect many times that.

The next time Jeff Crowley went into town with his truck, Dade caught a ride with him. He bought a quantity of poultry netting and some fencing staples, which Jeff obligingly unloaded right at the door of the three-room cabin where he lived. For the next few days Dade was busy.

In the forest he cut a number of black cherry trees, and split the trunks with a maul and wedges until he had a sufficient supply of lumber. The ground was frozen much too hard even to think of digging post holes, so Dade nailed cherry sticks together for a foundation, fastened uprights to them, and then laid sticks across the top until he had a framework fifteen feet wide by thirty long. Over the frame he stretched and stapled poultry netting.

When he was finished he had a big cage with a small wooden door at the far end, a door held shut by a hasp that clamped over a U latch. An ordinary iron bolt, dropped through the U, kept the door from swinging open.

With painstaking care Dade examined his cage. He looked at every splice and every staple, strengthening and reinforcing where he thought such was needed. Finally satisfied that he had built a prison from which no fox could escape, he started on the next step of the campaign he had laid out.

Most foxes are sagacious creatures, possessed of a cunning intelligence matched by few other animals and surpassed by none. Nobody knew that better than Dade Matson. But Dade knew also that few foxes can match the cunning of a human being who understands them and their ways.

Dade did know, and so now he proceeded with extreme care. He had already de-scented his fox traps in boiling water to which had been added the bark of certain trees and a few other ingredients that Dade had discovered. Heavy trapping gloves he hung in the cold wind for a week, and boots beside them. A thirty-foot strip of canvas and his packsack were also hung out to weather, and even the axe he used to stake fox traps was de-scented.

When all was ready, he continued as carefully as a surgeon goes about a complicated operation. He went outside, slipped his hands into the gloves, kicked his moccasins off, and used the gloved hands to draw his boots on. Carefully, not permitting any part of them to touch his hands or coat, and so pick up human scent, he lifted the traps into his pack-sack, laid the roll of canvas on top of them, and set out.

He knew that foxes like to run trails, and his first

stop was to make a trail set. Dade unrolled the strip of canvas, walked on it to where he wanted the trap, excavated a hole with his axe, set the trap, staked it to a small limb, and covered it again. Then a broken bough was so placed that it looked as though the wind had carried it here. But any fox running this trail, and jumping over the bough, was sure to land in Dade's trap.

Rolling up the canvas behind him as he left, Dade was satisfied. No trace of scent lingered about the trap and no eye could have told that there was a trap there. It was a set that could have been made only by a master trapper who knew exactly what he was doing.

Dade's next was a water set. Coming to an unfrozen runlet that trickled from a small spring, he waded up it. With gloved hands he pried a stone loose from the bottom of the runlet and dropped it into the center of the spring, so that it protruded above water. On this he placed a couple of drops of scent which he himself, after many years of experimentation, had perfected. It was a mixture of fish oil, beaver castor, or the scent glands from beaver, and various other things which Dade knew would tempt foxes. Tying a small stone to the pan of his trap, he set it so that the small stone was between the rock in the center and the shore line, and also protruding above the water.

Foxes are not averse to water, but in zero

weather they are no more inclined to wade in it than anything with sense might be. A wandering fox, catching scent of the lure Dade had left on the stone in the center of the spring, would be tempted to investigate. So doing, it would place its paw on what appeared to be a small, convenient stepping stone—and land squarely in the waiting trap.

All that day, all the next, and all the day after, Dade set traps. On the fourth day he set out to see what he had caught.

The first trap, the one he had set in the trail, held a wildly struggling young fox. Unceremoniously Dade clubbed it over the head, re-set the trap, and went two hundred yards away to skin his catch. The thin, naked carcass he cast aside for carrion eaters.

The next three traps were untouched, but the one after that held a slim little vixen who, by crouching close to the ground and not moving, hoped to escape her tormentor's notice. Dade's eyes lighted with pleasure. The vixens were what he really wanted.

He looped a rope over her neck, stretched her out with the trap on one foot, and worked his hands down the rope until he could grasp her around the neck. Dade tied her feet, muzzled her jaws with stout cord, and dropped her into the packsack.

Two more vixens he caught that day, and both of them he took alive. All three in his packsack, he carried them back to his cabin, untied the ropes that bound them, and freed them in the cage. That was his plan. He would catch as many vixens as he could, feed them on venison that he could get for nothing in the woods anyway, and wait for their cubs to be born. Then he would collect a bounty on mother and cubs alike, and by keeping just one fox alive for a sufficient length of time he would collect from five to nine bounties.

Dade knew that he might run into trouble. Even foxes that have been penned for generations want no human near when it is time for their young to be born. But Dade decided that he could take care of any difficulties that might arise.

As the season wore on, Dade left his cabin two hours before daylight and never got back to it until after nightfall. His plan was succeeding. The pelts of twenty-six foxes, mostly spring cubs but with a few old dogs among them, hung in his drying room. Twenty-one vixens due to produce young crawled fearfully about the cage, and at night quarreled over the venison Dade gave them to eat.

Soon, Dade knew, he would no longer be able to run his traps but must stay home to watch his penned females. However, since each one should be worth from twenty to forty dollars in bounty money alone, Dade felt that he could afford to watch them. He allotted himself one more day of trapping.

On that day, in a lonely thicket which had looked

to Dade like a good blind set, he took Star's mate in
one of his traps.

It was a sinister trap, set in a trail leading to one
of Vixen's favorite rabbit thickets. It was a lonely,
winding path, used exclusively by foxes, rabbits,
deer, and other wild things. Twisting through scrub
hemlocks, among tumbled boulders, and beside
snarled patches of laurel, it was not a path that men
would ordinarily choose. Few men even knew
about it. Dade Matson knew, and he had come to
the trail so carefully that not one of the wild things
whose highway it was was aware that he had been
there.

With early evening Star and Vixen bestirred
themselves from the thicket in which they had been
sleeping and padded down the path. At first Star
trotted ahead of his mate. But he halted when the
night wind brought to his nostrils the scent of roosting turkeys, and as he stood with one fore paw
raised, trying to determine the turkeys' exact location, Vixen brushed impatiently past him and ran on
ahead. She had tried and failed to catch turkeys
before, and because of that had little interest in
them.

Vixen leaped over a knotty stick that looked as
though it had fallen from a half-dead tree, and
thrust her delicate front paw squarely into one of

the waiting traps. There was a metallic snap in the night, as the trap leaped from its hiding place to clamp Vixen well up on her left front paw. Reacting instantly, she tried to spring away.

She was jerked to a sudden stop by the trap's three-foot chain, and flew head over heels to land facing in the opposite direction. The suddenly taut chain dragged across the pan of the set's second trap, and that, too, snapped. But all it seized was the chain. Vixen made another wild, surging leap to the side and her shoulder pulled painfully. Again swapping ends, she was brought to a jolting halt.

Losing her first, blind fear, Vixen lay full length on the snow, easing the tension of the tight trap chain. Gravely she studied the trap, then lifted her head to touch noses with Star, who had moved up beside her and was standing worriedly near. He stretched on the snow, facing her, while both inspected the trap. It was a dangerous and deadly thing and both knew it. Star touched the trap with his nose, and when nothing happened he examined it thoroughly. Gently he licked Vixen's imprisoned paw.

Limping on three legs, carrying the trap on her upraised fourth paw, Vixen rose and stalked very carefully away. It was no use; the trap followed her wherever she went and stopped her when she came to the end of the chain. She did not strain and jump because she had already learned that so doing only brought more pain and did not help free her. Again she lay down to study the trap.

While Star, his ears pricked forward, looked anxiously on, she tried cutting it with her teeth. Her fangs made a scraping noise in the still night, and scarred the trap with silvery streaks, but it did not yield the least bit. Obviously it could not be torn with teeth.

Star picked the chain up in his teeth, but when he put pressure on Vixen's paw, she whimpered. Star dropped the chain, studied it a moment, and used his front paws to scratch a trench in the snow. With his nose he nudged the trap chain into the trench and scraped snow over it. Then he walked a few feet to the side of the trail and called Vixen to him. She came, but when she did the trap came too, pulling the chain out of the snow. When she reached the chain's limits, Vixen whined in pain and sat down again.

Star crept forward to comfort her, and for a while they lay side by side, regarding the trap with worried eyes. Every time a breeze stirred, or another animal moved, or a nightfaring bird's wings rustled, Star was on his feet and ready to fight. Though he was unable to help Vixen in her hour of trial, he was wholly willing and ready to defend her should an enemy come. None came.

Dawn rose slowly in a sky piled high with scattered banks of clouds that carried a threat of more snow to come. Presently the first few flakes drifted quietly down, then more and more.

Star walked anxiously back and forth. His belly was empty; he had eaten nothing since the day before. But he would not go forth to hunt while Vixen was trapped and unable to run with him. She lay prone in the gathering snow, not moving because every motion brought pain. She had tried every way she knew to fight the trap and nothing worked.

The stiff breeze blew from the valley up the path, and brought the odors of many things. Star recoiled and sniffed deeply as one odor, rising above all the rest, came powerfully to his keen nostrils. Dade Matson was coming up the trail.

Vixen smelled him too, and flattened herself on the snow with her front paws straight before her and her rear ones outstretched. She pressed her head close to the trail and lay motionless, fearing the man's scent more than anything else. Dade's odor freshened as he came nearer.

Not until Dade was almost upon them did Star slip away, and then he went only a few yards into the brush. He was tense, alert; and afraid. Any wilderness enemy that approached would have found him by Vixen's side, battling for her, but this foe he dared not face. He crouched out of sight, trusting to his marvelous nose and keen ears to tell him of Vixen's fate.

He heard the sound of Dade's rubber-bottomed

pacs crunching the lightly crusted snow, and Vixen's scent came warmly to him. Then the odors of fox and man intermingled. Star's mate did not growl or snarl. Had Star but known it, she was still plastered flat against the snow, watching Dade with quick eyes. Only when the looping rope settled around her neck did she struggle, and then it was not a prolonged effort. The tightening rope choked her, the trap pinched her paw cruelly as Dade stretched her out. She felt his hands on her neck, then the binding ropes around her muzzle and paws.

His prize secure, Dade looked around and a wolfish grin crossed his lips as he read the tracks in the fresh snow. Until now he hadn't been sure whether or not the famous Haunt Fox still lived or had succumbed to rabies. But Star's distinctive paw prints were all around the traps, and Dade knew that he must have left his imprisoned mate unwillingly and at the last possible moment. Even now he probably was not very far away. But there was little use in looking for him. The Haunt Fox was too smart to show himself.

Dumping Vixen unceremoniously into his packsack, Dade picked up his traps and started back down the trail.

As soon as he considered it safe to do so, Star followed. He did not stay directly on Dade's trail but clung to the brush at one side, letting the wind

bring to him the story of Dade and the captive
Vixen. Dade came out of the brush into a forest of
big trees and Star trod more warily. In heavy brush
he could slip away as silently as a ghost, but here
among trees it was much harder to hide completely.
Though boughs and twigs were so thickly interlaced
that they overspread the whole forest floor, there
were wide spaces between the trunks. With the
snow as background, Star could be seen slipping
from trunk to trunk, and he knew it.

The trees ended a few rods from the clearing in
which Dade's cabin was built, and Star stopped
short. He padded restlessly back and forth in the
still falling snow until he found a wind current that
was blowing directly from Dade's place. Then he
settled himself at the base of a big tree and continued to read with his nose the story of what was
taking place.

All the odors that are customarily found about any
structure inhabited by humans drifted to his questing nostrils. There was the smell of wood smoke,
the lingering odors of cooked food, refuse. Star located Dade's two hounds, that were chained to kennels, and smelled the restless, worried, nervous she
foxes. Mingled with their odors was that of Vixen.
From out of the cabin came Dade's scent.

Back toward the head of the hollow a deep-voiced
hound began to sing out his discovery of a fresh fox
track. Star recognized Thunder's voice, but he did

not worry. Though he was well aware of the fact that he left tracks wherever he went, not in a long while had he been in the place from which Thunder was tonguing now. The big black and tan hound must be on the trail of another fox.

Though Star was hungry, he was too troubled and anxious to do any hunting. All day he lingered as close as he dared to the pen in which Vixen was one of many prisoners. When night came he grew bolder, and cautiously trotted toward the cage.

Well inside Dade's clearing, Star halted again. The chained hounds paid no attention to him. Though they were hunting dogs, there were so many foxes in the cage that they had become used to and slightly bored with them. Star smelled Dade Matson, asleep in the cabin, and swerved aside.

He walked on padded paws that made not even a whisper of noise, but Vixen was there to meet him when he pushed his pointed nose against the cage's tough wire. The rest of the trapped foxes hung back, suspicious of everything, including males of their own kind.

Star raised a black paw to push at the wire. It bent before his prodding foot, but when he withdrew his paw the wire sprang right back into place again. Dejectedly Vixen sat down, watching her mate, but when he started around the outside of the cage she followed him on the inside.

Every inch of the cage Star inspected, seeking a

break or a weak spot where he might make a hole that would allow Vixen to escape. There were none. Dade Matson knew what it took to hold foxes and had built accordingly. A dozen times, slowly and patiently, Star circled the cage. Then, realizing the hoplessness of breaking in or of letting Vixen out from any place on the ground, he turned his attention elsewhere.

The cage was four feet high. Across the tops of the supporting posts were black cherry poles, which had been spliced together to make them long enough. Poultry netting was stretched over the top of the cage, too, in order to prevent the foxes from jumping out.

Again Star trotted around the cage, but now his head was raised as he sought a way to spring to the top. The gate offered the best way up, and in a single graceful leap, Star cleared the ground. He caught himself with his front paws, pushing on the gate with his rear ones as he scrambled to a cross bar and supported himself there. But when he tried to walk across the top of the cage, the netting sagged under his weight and made him afraid.

When the first streaks of dawn broke the night sky, Star reluctantly left Vixen and trotted back into the forest. An hour later, in the new snow, Dade Matson read all about his visit.

Dade had expected some dog foxes to come in search of their trapped mates, but up until now none had. But the Haunt Fox had come. Dade grinned. Whoever pulled the Haunt Fox's pelt over a stretching board would have reason to boast. Dade made preparations to receive Star should he come back.

Instead of going to bed that night, he sat before a partly opened window, facing the cage. In his hands, its muzzle thrust through the window, was a single-barreled, ten-gauge shotgun loaded with Number 2 shot. The thin sickle of a moon rode high, faintly illuminating the tops of trees and other objects but leaving the ground in shadow. A half hour after he took up his vigil, Dade saw Star.

Again he was circling the cage. Dade tensed, ready finger on the shotgun's trigger. Moonlight slanted across the cage, lighting up the side toward the house, the side upon which the gate hung, but leaving everything else dark. Star, moving about the cage, was very hard to see and Dade wanted to be sure before he shot. He wanted the Haunt Fox, but one shot was all he would have and he did not want to miss.

Star came around the end of the cage, into the moonlight, and Dade scarcely breathed. The Haunt Fox was his any time he chose to take him, but Dade held his fire. On the inside of the cage, Vixen was keeping as close to Star as she could get and Dade didn't want to kill her, too. He waited for Star to move away from Vixen, or for her to leave his side.

Suddenly Dade realized that Star was going to jump to the top of the cage. The fox was almost invisible in the dark shadow of the gate, but without being able to see him clearly, Dade knew what he was doing. He was measuring the distance to the top, tensing his muscles to leap again. Dade shifted the shotgun slowly, bringing its muzzle up a trifle and squarely in line with the gate. When Star was off the ground, Dade could shoot and get him without hitting any of the others. He saw a shadow go up and pressed the trigger. Flame belched from the shotgun's muzzle and there was the sound of shotgun pellets tearing into wood. Feverishly Dade sought in his pocket for a second shell.

The shadow he had seen was just that, a shadow born of the capricious moonlight. Though Dade had moved his shotgun very slowly and carefully, Star had still detected the sound. Instead of leaping he had waited to find out what it was and where it came from. Dade's full charge of shot had ripped into the hasp that held the gate closed, and torn it off. The gate swung open, and now there were many flitting shadows in the moonlight.

Before Dade could reload the shotgun, the cage was empty.

Chapter 9  The Den

Star stayed close behind Vixen, urging her into the forest. For a little way two of the other freed foxes ran with them, then veered off in a direction of their own choosing and left Star and Vixen to travel on alone.

The baying of Dade's two hounds rose in the snowy night air. Not knowing what else to do, hoping to recapture at least one of his escaped prisoners, Dade had set them free to hunt. Star paid no attention because he was not afraid of Dade's hounds. Besides, both of them had taken the track of another fox, and their voices were fading in the distance. Star slowed to an easy trot.

As soon as she sensed that Star had slowed up, Vixen paused, too. She was nervous and tense, mentally upset by her experience in the cage, but save for her trap-pinched paw, none the worse for it. Vixen waited for Star to come up beside her. They sniffed noses, and Star licked her cheek with a warm, gentle tongue. When they traveled on, he took the lead.

A soft south wind had sprung up and the new snow, the season's last, turned slushy under their paws. Creeks that had been ice-locked now had water seeping over the ice. In the more sheltered places, willows were heavy with buds and needed only a few warm days before they would be fluffy with mitten-shaped pussy willows.

The trap in the trail, whose presence had been suspected by neither himself nor his mate until she was caught in it, had taught Star something. When he came to another thin little trail, one that under ordinary circumstances he would have followed, he jumped over it instead and Vixen followed. With absolute confidence in his woods sense, she waited for him to decide before making any moves herself. At no time did she want to be far from his side. For an hour, jumping over trails and keeping in the forest or brush, Star led her straight away from Dade Matson's. Then, about to jump another trail, he smelled a trap.

It was not one of Dade Matson's sets, but one that

Eli Catman had put out to protect his rabbits. The trap was poorly set and had not been properly deodorized. Both Eli's scent and the trap would have been evident to even a dull-nosed fox. To Star's sharpened senses, the trap's location was plain.

Very slowly, exactly sure of where he placed each black paw, Star walked toward it. From a distance of four feet he inspected it with his nose, and drooled at the scent with which the trap had been baited. It was an alluring odor, and under ordinary circumstances Star would have investigated it thoroughly. But evidences of man, and of the same sort of trap into which Vixen had fallen, erected a solid wall beyond which he would not go.

Very slowly, still being careful of where he placed each paw, Star circled the trap so that he could investigate it from every possible angle. Finally, in a sudden fit of anger, he turned and used his rear paws to scrape snow and dirt over it. The little cascade of frozen dirt arched over the trap, and Star leaped in quick surprise when the trap sprang, making a metallic snap.

Nothing else happened, and Star turned again to look at the trap. Thrown from its bed by the swift closing of its own springs, it lay on top of the snow, its chain sagging limply beside it. Without going any nearer. Star stretched his neck and sniffed cautiously.

Thus he added to his education knowledge that would enable him to keep alive. Traps were dangerous, but only at extremely close ranges. They could not reach very far to strike, and they could be forced to reveal themselves by having trash scratched over them. The scent used to bait traps Star remembered, and he would always remember. It was an enchanting lure, but it could lead only to disaster. In Star's mind it became a danger signal.

They stopped in a thicket to hunt, caught rabbits, and Star enjoyed his first meal since Vixen had been trapped. Ordinarily he would have lain down to sleep after eating, but now he did not because he was still worried. He had long since learned that guile and speed would serve him much better than strength, and every sense within him cried that he must get farther away from Dade Matson.

The night turned colder, and the soft snow froze underfoot. Star led Vixen to a small, unfrozen stream which he had intended to wade, but he hesitated to enter because it was cold. Instead he sought a boulder-strewn slope and, with his mate beside him, climbed up over the big stones, leaping from one to another. Melting snow had left the tops of the boulders bare, and the foxes left no visible trail.

With daylight, high on top of one of the hills, they rested in a thicket. Vixen slept soundly. Star, who had been careful to seek their bed where the wind carried to them from their back trail, was wakeful.

But all that day nothing threatened them and with night they went forth to hunt again.

Because Star had done no back-tracking, he did not know that Dade Matson had been on his trail. Two hours before dawn his hounds had returned, and were lying beside the door when Dade went out. He was beside himself with anger because he had lost all the penned foxes, and his rage vented itself in Star's direction. Had the Haunt Fox never come, the vixens never would have escaped.

From the many fox trails in the snow, Dade finally singled out those left by Star and Vixen. His hounds on leash, Dade tracked them through the snow but lost them in the boulders over which Star had led his mate. Dade urged his hounds to cast about for Star's trail, but they refused. Already they had run a good share of the night, and the only trail that might have tempted them now would have been a very fresh one.

Knowing that he had lost his victims, Dade took the hounds back to his cabin. Tying the dogs to their kennels, Dade went to work on his fox traps. Now it was a personal issue; for the first time in his life Dade wanted to take an animal for something besides money. If he never did another thing in his life, he vowed, he would pull Star's pelt over a stretching board.

Leaving the hounds at home, Dade set out to

string more fox traps. This time he wanted only one fox.

Far back in the hills, Vixen refused to be lured out of the deepest and most impenetrable thickets, and because she was contented in such places, Star was satisfied to stay at her side. The hunting was good and there was plenty of cover. Enemies could not find them.

As the last of the snows melted and feathery buds uncurled, Vixen became ill-tempered and snappish. Once she even walked up to Star and snatched from his jaws a rabbit he had caught. She was a new and uncertain mate, one Star had never known before, and because he was now a little bit afraid of her, Star let her have her way.

Vixen was also interested in new and strange places. She never passed an old woodchuck den, a crevice, or even a hollow stump, without stopping to investigate it thoroughly. When Star would have looked, too, she turned on him with lifted lips and snarling jaws. Though Star did not know it, Vixen was hunting a home den.

Together they traveled through the hills, and one early spring night when the air was spicy with the scent of new and growing things, they came among the boulders and to the fissure where, long ago, Star had waited out the first storm of winter. The leaning stone was still in place, hiding the fissure's mouth.

The porcupine was gone. Three hundred yards from the leaning stone, the querulous old beast hung clumsily in the crotch of a birch tree and let spring warmth drive the winter aches from its aging joints. Only in winter did the porcupine want shelter. All through the spring and summer winds, rains, and sun, it would spend its time in the trees.

Vixen slipped behind the leaning stone and into the fissure. By this time uncomfortably aware that she did not want him along when she inspected den sites, Star waited with his tail curled around his rear paws and his front feet shifting nervously. Vixen reappeared, stood a second looking around, and ducked back into the fissure.

It was another hour before she rejoined Star, and when she did a strange tension and anxiety gripped her. Forty feet from the leaning stone she sat obstinately down, looking back over her shoulder. When she finally did consent to hunt she walked only a little way. Star coaxed her with little whines and pleading manner. He knew of better hunting grounds, but she would have none of them. Vixen seemed to have lost all interest in hunting; when a mouse rustled almost beside her she did not even turn her head to look.

Rearing, Star pinned the mouse between his front paws and probed with his slim muzzle at the pile of grass and sticks that he had caught with the mouse. He held the tiny creature between his teeth, looking questioningly at Vixen. She snarled, and Star hastily ate his catch.

A half hour later, when he leaped to bring down a grouse that whirred in startled flight from the lower branches of a tree, she approached without any hesitation, took the grouse from his jaws, and ran back toward the bluffs. Crouching, she held the grouse with her front paws, plucked it, and ate. When he would have come to her side, she drove him back with slashing teeth and fierce snarls. Then Vixen slipped behind the leaning rock into the fissure, and did not come out again.

Star waited outside, troubled and mystified. While the wind rippled his fur, he curled up with his head on his paws. But he did not sleep. His mate's behavior was too disturbing. Finally tired of waiting, he went behind the leaning rock, only to have fury explode about him. It was Vixen, every hair on her body erect as, with slashing teeth, she flung herself upon her mate. Star beat an undignified retreat, and went hunting for himself.

In the light gray hours of early dawn he padded back to the fissure. Vixen was his mate, and in spite of her recent savage manner, Star would not even think of leaving her. He halted a safe distance from the leaning stone and sat down. Nothing happened, so he sneaked cautiously up to the fissure.

Vixen lay within, flat on her side, while Star's three sons and two daughters scrambled blindly over her and sought with soft mouths for the life-giving milk she furnished. Heeding Vixen's warning snarl, Star did not try to enter, but retreated to a little cluster of laurel about twenty feet from the leaning rock. He curled up beneath the laurel, his head on his flank and bushy tail covering nose and paws.

He slept for only an hour. Since Vixen could not or would not do her own hunting, Star must do it for her. He glided away, laid an ambush where he knew grouse fed, and caught one.

He was carrying the grouse back to Vixen when he detected Dade Matson's scent, and bristled with fear. Dade was their deadly enemy, and Vixen was helpless in the fissure. Star paused, undecided as to what to do. Then he raced back to the fissure, dis-covered that Dade had not been there, and left the grouse. Without stopping, he set out to find just where Dade was and what he was doing.

Star found the scent where the trapper had struck cross-country between two trails, and followed at a slow walk. He did not stay right on Dade's trail, but walked to one side and never put a paw down with-out knowing exactly where he was putting it. Dade left traps behind him, and Star had had grim experi-ence with traps.

Not until he came directly upon a trail did he find the first trap. Cleverly set, even a wise fox might have stepped into it if he had not been looking for such a thing. Star was looking. He expected a trap, and it was a patch of freshly disturbed grass that warned him of its presence. Dade had scooped a hole with the blade of his axe and set his trap carefully in it, but he had not been able to replace the green grass so that it was an exact match for the rest.

As soon as he was sure of its location, Star investigated. There was the usual stick in the trail, so placed that it looked as through the wind had blown it there. But there was no man scent around. Dade's trail led to within thirty feet of the trap and broke suddenly. Circling, Star discovered that the trail began again thirty feet beyond. The sixty-foot break where no break should have been excited his interest, and he went back to the trap.

For a while he sat still, looking at the set, then he turned his back to it and scraped vigorously with his rear paws. A little rain of dirt and pebbles cascaded over the traps. Star heard the metallic snap he had expected to hear, and turned to look. Now the sprung trap lay fully exposed in the trail.

Tongue showing between partly open jaws, a light of mischief dancing in his eyes, Star trotted back into the brush and picked up Dade's trail. He found and sprung another trap. From the second set, Dade had swung back down into the valley and Star followed the trail clear out of his hunting range. Only then was he satisfied to return to Vixen.

Star could not know it, but Dade's thirst for revenge was as strong as ever, and even when he went root hunting he carried a couple of fox traps and set them wherever he thought they might do some good. It was a haphazard, blind search with no snow to aid him, and Dade hadn't the least idea where Star and Vixen were living.

However, the next time he looked at the traps Star had sprung, he was reasonably sure that he had again located the Haunt Fox. Not forgotten was the trap Star had sprung while there was still snow on the ground, and then his tracks had marked him plainly. Though other foxes will spring traps in such a fashion, not many of them ever learn the trick. Therefore, whenever he could, Dade went into Star's hunting range. He set no more traps because he did not want Star to find and spring them. His purpose now was to locate the den and cubs.

Occasionally Star ran across Dade's trail and followed it. He had taught himself what to look for, but he found no more traps and paid no special attention to the man. As yet, Dade had not been near the den again.

Star's hunting territory was well defined, not by any special feature of terrain, but where it joined the ranges of other foxes. So far all had found good hunting and there had been no reason to intrude on each other's home country. If the game played out in their own territory they would not hesitate to trespass, but if they did and were detected they would also have to fight.

Other wanderers went freely wherever they wished to go. Star followed a black bear with three cubs clear across his home range, and left their trail only when they left his country. He knew the location of every weasel, marten, and fisher. There were very few of these last and for the most part they stayed in deep woods, but weasels were numerous and sometimes they came near the fissure. Star attacked furiously whenever they did, and though he never caught a weasel he drove them into cracks and crevices, away from the den. He never went far to hunt when he knew a weasel was in the vicinity and was never satisfied until he had harried it away. Weasels were bloody little killers, and could easily cut a baby fox's throat.

There was one other enemy, a foe as dangerous as Dade Matson and as hated, that Star had not met in months. Stub, the surly wild cat, had also gone to the other side of the watershed while the summer madness raged. Finding good hunting there, Stub had remained throughout the season. Now, due largely to his depredations, there was not nearly as much game and hunting was hard. Stub came back on Star's side of the hills.

Star found his fresh trail one mellow night when he was out seeking food for Vixen. He bristled, and stiffened, while all the hate he had ever felt for the murderer of his brother welled up in him. At top speed Star flew along the trail, his heart beating fast. Stub was heading directly toward the bluff where Vixen lay with her cubs.

The fox was still twenty yards away when he heard Vixen's rippling snarl. Star gave a mighty leap that carried him within sight of the leaning rock, and in the dim moonlight he saw Stub. Short tail erect, the wild cat was tense and stiff. Between him and the fissure was Vixen, her slim body straight and her fangs bared as she prepared to give her own life rather than let harm come to her babies. At once Star attacked.

He flashed in from the rear, and because his arrival was a complete surprise he sliced twice with his teeth before Stub whirled away. The wild cat leaped to a small rock, spitting his rage, then sprang at Star. Up he went, front paws outspread and snarling mouth open as he sought to pin the fox in his tracks. But Star was more agile than Stub, and wise enough to know that, if the cat caught him, it would be the end. When Stub came down, Star was not there.

The fox slithered to one side, swift as a snake, and leaped in again to slash. Star tasted blood in his mouth, and knew that it was not his own. He danced on his rear paws, slapping with his front ones like a boxer, keeping just out of reach, waiting for his chance. His eyes were on Stub's soft belly, and at the right moment, he closed.

He felt his teeth sink deep through fur and muscle. Stub snarled his pain and anger, arched his back to strike, and hit out with both front paws. Dodging away from one, Star ran squarely into the other. He felt the piercing needles that were Stub's claws burn through his skin and into his ribs. He heard Stub's throaty growl of satisfaction as the wild cat began to pull the fox within reach of his jaws.

Star braced his feet, and did as much damage as he could with slashing jaws. But the wild cat was bigger than he and far stronger. Inch by inch, Star yielded. He could not resist the supple strength of Stub, but not for a second did he stop fighting.

Then, suddenly, he was free. Vixen, who had the courage of a pit bull when her cubs were endangered, had anxiously watched the battle between her mate and Stub. Forgotten by both, who had no time to think of anything save each other, she suddenly sprang clear from the mouth of the den and chopped twice. Vixen knew how to strike, and her jaws were strong.

Stub sagged on rear paws that would no longer obey him. Vixen had cut the tendons, the heavy control cords, and Stub's rear legs were useless. Star sprang in to strike again, while the wild cat was off guard, and struck well. Bright blood bubbled down Stub's velvet-furred neck. Tenacious and tough-bodied, Stub dragged himself with his front paws. Ten feet he went, then ten yards, while Star hovered at his side, waiting to get in the final blow. He did not have to. Stub marshalled his fading strength for one last effort, trying to drag himself to the top of a flat rock. Scrambling with his front paws, he climbed part way up, faltered, rolled from the rock, and lay unmoving in its shadow.

Chapter 10  Dade Matson

Dade Matson was a moody man and, like many of his kind, more than a little given to superstition. He believed, for one thing, that the various phases of the moon have a profound influence on human beings and conducted himself accordingly. If he set his traps and did not take as much fur as he thought he should, the moon was wrong. It was the same with fishing, root hunting, or anything else Dade happened to be doing. If the results were not good, they would be as soon as the moon was right again, and in his favor.

Now he blamed ill-timed phases of the moon for lack of success in his personal feud with the Haunt

Fox. Dade had hunted long and hard for even a faint
sign of Star. The deliberately sprung traps made
him positive that they had been set in the Haunt
Fox's hunting grounds. Because he knew foxes,
Dade could calculate with reasonable certainty the
probable limits of Star's range, and had traveled the
area time after time. He knew every woodchuck
hole, every hollow stump, and almost every tree in
it. He had visited the den where Star was born, and
found it uninhabited this season. But, after going to
every place he knew, Dade had still not found the
slightest trace of a fox's den or cubs.

The one place he had not looked was the fissure
behind the leaning rock, and the reason was because it was the one place he did not know. He had
crossed the tumble of boulders several times, but
the leaning stone, looking like another boulder,
concealed the opening behind it. Shrubs and brush
had grown up on both sides, making additional
camouflage. Furthermore, only scattered trees and
copses of brush grew in the rock patch. Foxes liked
brush in which they could hide, and it seemed most
unlikely that they would stay among boulders, particularly with young cubs to conceal.

The fact that Dade knew the country where Star's
den was located, and was still unable to find the
den, served only to deepen his conviction that the
moon was at fault. Until now it had been the fox's

moon, with everything in Star's favor. But that couldn't last.

Dade could not give all his time to the hunt because he had to harvest the medicinal roots which furnished him with most of his summer's income. Ginseng and golden seal he sought most eagerly because they brought the highest prices. In addition to them, Dade dug a number of other roots which he sorted, dried, and sold to the storekeeper in the little town of Carneyville, the valley's nearest shopping center. When he had enough roots to sell, he could usually get a ride with one of the farmers. If nobody happened to be going in, and Dade wanted to market his roots, he loaded them on a sturdy four-wheeled cart he had built and pulled them three miles to the store.

The late afternoon was hot and dusty. Pulling his empty cart, Dade was returning from the store, intending to go home. But as he approached the Crowley farm he changed his mind. If he stopped he could certainly get a drink of water or cold buttermilk, and probably he would be invited to share the evening meal.

As Dade pulled his wagon up the drive and left it, Thunder wagged lazily from the lilac thicket. Dade petted the big hound with a certain annoyance. He knew Thunder not only as the best hound in the valley but one of the best he had ever seen, and he resented the fact that such a dog was owned by a boy who wanted to hunt only for sport. To Dade that seemed an incredibly silly thing. Fox hunting was hard work, so why do it unless you expected to be paid for it or unless, as in the case of the Haunt Fox, it was a personal feud?

Thunder, listless with the heat, ambled back to the cool hole he had scraped in the lilac thicket. Mrs. Crowley came to the door.

"Hello, Dade," she said.

"Hello, Mrs. Crowley. Are your men folk around?"

"They're still working. Come on into the kitchen. It's cooler; I have the fan going."

"No thanks," Dade declined. "I'll go see if I can give 'em a hand."

He walked toward the barn, not because he wanted to work, but because if he helped with the chores he would almost certainly be invited for supper. Mrs. Crowley was a superb cook, and like most men who live alone, Dade was usually tired of his own cooking. He found Jeff in the barn, about to unhitch his team of work horses. Jack was going down the lane to drive the lagging cows up to be milked.

"Hi, Jeff," Dade said cordially. "Want me to take care of the horses?"

"Sure. If you want to."

Expertly Dade uncoupled the two big horses, and

of their own accord each went into the barn and
sought its separate stall. Dade followed, stripped off
the harnesses and hung them on the harness pegs.
With a currycomb and brush he groomed the
powerful beasts while they sighed with pleasure.
Dade went into the loft to pitch hay down, and gave
the horses what he knew was their proper measure
of grain.

By the time he was finished, Jack and Jeff were
milking. Dade quenched his thirst at the barn
spigot and sat down on an empty nail keg. Jack
emptied his foaming pail of milk into one of the big
cans in the cooler, and a moment later Jeff followed
him. Both sat down on milking stools and resumed
their work.

"How's it going, Dade?" Jeff asked companion-
ably.

Dade bit his words off. "Not good! The moon's
been against me! But it'll change and then I'll nail
that Ha'nt Fox!"

Their attention caught by the viciousness behind
Dade's words, Jack and Jeff turned to stare curiously at him. Neither could understand hatred of an
animal.

"Have you got a line on him?" was all Jeff said.

"He's up in the hills around Colt Hollow; that
much I know! Twenty-one vixens due to whelp he
cost me! I'll get him if I never do another thing!"

Dade had told and re-told of Star's raid on his

cage of trapped females, and the story had aroused new interest in the Haunt Fox. Most of the valley residents hadn't liked Dade's scheme to kill helpless cubs born in a cage, and had been secretly pleased when the foxes escaped. And in Dade's feud with Star, sympathies leaned in favor of the Haunt Fox. Not that anyone who liked to hunt would miss a chance to shoot Star if he could do it. But all knew of Dade's skill and methods, and felt that Star could not fail to go down if Dade hunted him hard enough. Consequently, the fox had won the sympathy usually felt for the underdog in any contest.

They finished milking, washed their faces, hands, and arms at the barn spigot, and went to the house for supper. Tired after a hard day in the fields, Jack and Jeff talked little. Dade, too busy eating to do anything else, talked only when he was spoken to. The Haunt Fox was not mentioned again. After eating, Dade took his leave and pulled the four-wheeled cart to his own cabin. There he fed his dogs, sat for a while staring out of the window into the gathering night, and went to bed.

The next morning he was awake with the dawn. He filled the hounds' dishes with water, made his breakfast, packed a lunch, slung a packsack over his shoulders, and started into the hills. Again he headed toward the place where Star had sprung his traps.

Roots, like gold, occurred where you found them.

More than once, after thinking that he had scouted a whole section thoroughly, Dade had pushed his way into some shady and hitherto unexplored thicket and found a whole patch of ginseng or golden seal. In spite of the fact that he had already spent a great deal of time in Star's home range, he felt justified in going there again.

All morning he hunted roots, but with only meager success. At noon he sat down to eat his lunch near a tumbled clutter of boulders. Dade lifted a sandwich to his mouth, but he did not take a bite out of it. He didn't even move. A hundred yards away, a big dog fox trotted lightly among and over the boulders. In his mouth he carried a half-grown rabbit.

Dade remained in his sitting position. The fox went to a leaning stone, dropped the rabbit, panted in the sun, and stole away to hunt again. Not until he had been gone for several minutes did Dade leave, and then he moved as silently as a shadow, directly away from the boulders. Only when he had put a quarter of a mile between himself and the boulders did he walk freely.

The moon had changed in his favor. He knew that he had seen Star and he also knew where the Haunt Fox had his den. Obviously the leaning stone concealed a cave or den. Dade could go down to it at once and catch Star's cubs and possibly his mate. But he wanted the Haunt Fox, too.

When the moon turned to his side, Dade thought with satisfaction, it turned completely. Prevailing summer winds blew over the boulders, toward the place where Dade had sat when he saw Star. The fox couldn't scent him. And it was only about a hundred yards from that place to the leaning stone. With his deer rifle, Dade could put six shots into a three-inch circle at a hundred yards. He couldn't possibly miss.

The next morning, two hours before dawn, he was back at the place where he had eaten his lunch. His deer rifle, loaded and with the safety off, lay across his knees. Dade hardly breathed as he waited for daylight to bring him the opportunity for which he had waited so long.

Star was thin, almost gaunt, and he was always hungry, hunting for two. Vixen had not yet permitted him to come into the fissure and she hadn't brought the cubs out; Star scarcely saw the family he worked so hard to feed. But as the cubs grew, which they did with unbelievable speed, their demands increased prodigiously. They took as much from Vixen as their stomachs could hold, and ten minutes later they were looking for more. Their constant demands were a ceaseless drain on Vixen, and in turn she had to look to Star.

The cubs had to grow fast if they were going to

learn everything that they should while the summer lasted, and be in a position to fend for themselves when winter came. They could scramble around now, but as yet were able to stand only on wobbly legs. Vixen couldn't leave them except for very short periods.

She was always alert for Star's return, and as soon as he came she seized and ate the food he brought her. Vixen ate enormous amounts, but she was always hungry, too, for she had five other mouths to feed. The food she ate was transformed into rich milk for the cubs, and they showed it. They were bigger, stronger, and more alert than most fox cubs their age. As usual, there was one outstanding among them. That was a little male marked like Star and with his father's extra toe on each front paw. Almost as soon as his eyes were open, and before he was able to walk, he crawled on exploring trips about the fissure. Though he never went more than a few feet, Vixen was forever having to drag him back into the fissure and he was an endless source of worry.

Now and again Vixen tore herself away from her family, but never for long, and she seldom went more than a few feet from the mouth of the fissure. There she played and ran a bit to exercise cramped muscles. But Vixen was a chronic worrier, always troubled about her cubs even when they were beside her. Her excursions to the world outside the fissure consisted of a bit of exercise, a few deep draughts of fresh air, and hasty gulps of water from the nearby stream.

Vixen was outside the fissure, and the cubs, for once, were sleeping, when, as softly as a ghost, Vixen's mate appeared beside her. Vixen backed away. There was within her a deep instinct that no living thing except herself must ever get close to the precious cubs. However, Star had not tried to come near them and she was no longer greeting him with snarls and bared fangs when he came. Had he wanted to, he probably could have entered the den. But not forgotten were her former savage attacks, and now he would not enter until he was invited.

Star dropped his offering, a muskrat, and for a brief moment the two touched noses. Then Vixen took the muskrat and carried it into the fissure with her. Star curled tiredly beneath the laurel where he had slept so many nights and rested with his head on outstretched paws. As usual, he slept lightly, alert to the stirring breeze. A half hour later he rose, stretched, and spread his jaws in a weary yawn.

For days now Star had ranged all about, at first within short distances of the den and then, as game grew scarce or hard to catch, going farther afield. But this time he had made so many trips, and brought so much back to Vixen, that his whole range was becoming depleted. Hunting was much harder, but the demand for food was far greater.

Skirting the boulders on another hunt, Star stopped at once when he caught Dade Matson's scent. He traced it, finding exactly where Dade had sat and where he had gone. Almost to the cabin in Hungry Hollow Star went. Finally satisfying himself that Dade was not in the hills now, he resumed his hunt.

He climbed the hill and went into thick laurel where snowshoe hares thumped the earth with their huge rear paws and hopped or raced down winding little trails. Snowshoes were notoriously hard to catch; when they called on all the speed they could muster they could outrun a fox. But there was always a possibility of ambushing or surprising one, and the first of the season's young, not nearly as wary as their elders, were now in evidence.

Star entered a thicket and trotted slowly along. His tail curved gracefully and his head was low. To all outward appearances he seemed wholly uninterested in what he would find. But his ears were alert and his nose was questing. He missed not the tiniest sound or the merest wisp of scent. He found, struck at, and missed a big hare that leaped away into the night. Star debated the advisability of trailing it, but decided against it. The hare was a powerful, strong-legged thing that might run for hours before it tired. It would be as easy to find and catch another as it would be to run this one down. Star continued his seemingly aimless trot through the thicket.

Suddenly he went into violent action.

Hearing and smelling a snowshoe that was nibbling grass near a fallen log, Star anticipated the way it would jump. Tail stiff behind him, jaws wide and ready to chop, he was there ahead of it. The snowshoe almost ran right into his waiting jaws, then doubled and raced back the other way. But Star instantly leaped, landing almost astride the fleeing hare, and before his paws touched the earth he had snapped. For a moment he panted over his quarry, then grasped it around the middle and lifted his head high. Carrying the hare, a big one and therefore a real prize, he started back toward Vixen.

He was still a long way off when he dropped his quarry and tensed. Forgetting all about the snowshoe, that had cost him so much time and effort, he trotted on and verified what his nose had already told him. Dade Matson had come back while Star hunted. Now he was sitting near the head of the boulders, in the same place where he had eaten his lunch.

Star trembled, nervous and terribly afraid. Chance might have brought Dade near the den once, but chance would not bring him twice. He had come back for a purpose, and it could not possibly be a good one. Soft-footed, Star made a wide circle around the waiting man, and came in to the den from the lower side. He was worried because he could no longer smell Dade, but there was nothing to indicate that the trapper might have moved.

The sky was a few shades lighter; daylight was not very far off. The wind continued to sweep up the valley, away from the fissure and toward the silent man crouching near the boulders.

Star went directly to the leaning stone, where the hungry Vixen met him. Bewildered because Star had brought nothing to eat, she fell back a step and looked steadily at him. Star paused, one front paw raised while he glanced back over his shoulder.

Neither one whined or made a sound. Save for the restlessly stirring cubs, the fissure was completely silent. Yet, something passed between Star and Vixen. In some way of his own he told her of the menace to their home, and she understood. She did not block his path, but trotted before him as he went over to look down at the cubs.

Huddled together for warmth, and still clothed in the fuzzy wool of babyhood, they looked more like tiny lambs than foxes. Star thrust a gentle nose toward them and the biggest cub, the one that looked most like him and had even inherited his father's extra toe, promptly bit him.

Star hesitated no longer. He grasped the furry

cub around the middle, held it loosely enough so that he would not hurt it but tightly enough not to drop it, and without looking behind carried it out of the fissure. Vixen followed with another cub.

In the pre-dawn darkness they ran swiftly but silently across the boulders and into thick brush on the other side. A mile from the den, they threaded their way into the center of a laurel patch. A great tree with spreading branches had once grown there. Years before Star's birth the tree had been blasted by lightning, and now all that was left was the withered, hollow stump and a few decaying boughs. Star and Vixen left the two cubs in the hollow stump and raced back to the den for another pair. Once they were safely in the stump, Vixen nestled beside the four, while Star faded into the laurel again.

Dawn had come. Trees and rocks were assuming definite shape. Twenty-five yards away, Star saw a feeding deer, and beyond it, a hawk spiraling into the sky.

One cub remained in the den, and Star had no thought of turning back. He ran until he came to the edge of the brush, then stopped for a moment to study the situation. Crouching, curving his tail around his rump and flattening his ears as he slunk behind a boulder, Star stalked to another boulder, keeping himself hidden. He came to the center of the stones and to a three-foot gap that he had to cross. His belly scraped the earth as Star wormed his way past the single aspen that grew in the gap.

Farther up, Dade Matson thought he saw a patch of reddish fur and tightened his hand about the rifle. Just at that moment a thrush flew into the tree and Dade decided that that was the motion he had seen.

Star reached the den, seized the cub, and retraced his dangerous path. Again, when he reached the gap, the watching man thought he saw something and fixed his eyes on that place. But the motion was not repeated.

Four hours later, weary of waiting, Dade Matson stalked cautiously down and discovered the fissure behind the leaning rock. But that was all he found.

Chapter 11  Wanderers

As soon as Star brought the last cub in, they moved again. With each parent carrying a baby, they trotted another mile to the bulging side of a great fallen tree. Leaving the two cubs there, they returned to the hollow stump for two more, then Vixen remained with the four while Star went to bring the remaining cub.

He put it in the leafy nest beside Vixen and left her at once. His mate was hungry and he knew it, but there was no time to stop and hunt. If she must have food she would have to get it herself. Though they were safe for the time being, at the very best

their safety was a temporary thing. Star knew that
Dade Matson had hounds which could trail them. It
was Star's place to put himself between his family
and anything that Dade Matson might do.

He snaked back to the pile of boulders, but this
time it was not necessary to take chances. Instead
he stayed in the brush, where he was well hidden
and where the wind could tell him what the man
was doing.

For a long while Dade did nothing. Finally he got
up and moved toward the fissure. Star stayed just
close enough to determine what he was doing. He
knew when Dade went behind the leaning stone
and looked into the fissure, when he found the body
of Stub, and when, at a fast walk that was almost a
trot, he started back toward his cabin.

Star trailed him, keeping in the brush at one side.
He did not venture among the open trees near
Dade's cabin, but waited in the brush to see what
the man would do. Ten minutes later Dade came
out of the cabin.

His shotgun in his hands, his two hounds on short
leashes, he strode purposefully back toward the fissure. Dade was furious. Yesterday he might have
taken the cubs, and probably the mate, too. By
delaying, hoping to get the Haunt Fox, he had lost
everything. Now he was determined to do as much
as he could to avenge that failure. He knew that the

cubs could not be far away. They would not be old enough to go anywhere by themselves and the parents must have carried them. At least he could find and kill the cubs. Dade went directly to the fissure.

Star followed, being careful not to show himself as the hounds cast about for scent. One of them bayed and strained forward as he found Vixen's trail. The other one, not as keen as his mate, pricked up his ears in lively interest. Then both tugged on the trail Vixen and Star had left. The leashes taut in his hand, Dade half-ran behind his dogs.

Star was worried. This was not what he had anticipated. He had expected the hounds to be loosed, the way dogs usually are when they run foxes, and then he would only have had to cut in ahead of them and lead them away. Now he dared not show himself. Dade traveled right with his dogs, and Star knew well the folly of letting himself be seen by a man with a gun.

Anxiously he shadowed them as the hounds led their master to the stump where Star and Vixen had first hidden their cubs. Dade inspected it carefully. Then he went on, toward the fallen tree beside which Vixen now lay. They had covered half the distance when Star got his chance.

He had been following on the downwind side, so that he might keep track of dogs and man, but now the wind changed. Star crossed the trail he had left earlier in the day and slunk into the brush on the opposite side. Thus, instead of a trail hours old, the hounds found one that was smoking hot.

While they were not the best hounds, they were still better than average. Their noses told them that they had been following the scent of two foxes, and that the foxes were carrying cubs, but they could not possibly know that their master wanted them to find the cubs. They did what any good dogs would have done, and left a cold trail for a fresh one which they knew had been laid by one of the two foxes they had been following.

Out in the brush Star heard them coming. This was what he had wanted; hounds and man following him. Staying downwind, Star trotted slowly along. He led the hounds in the straightest course he could away from Vixen and the cubs, and for two miles they followed.

Then Dade awakened to the fact that all was not as it should be. If the parent foxes had taken their cubs right out from under his nose this morning, as he was sure they had, they would not have been able to bring them this far.

Dade had purposely kept his dogs on leash because he was pretty sure that Star would be watching him, and Dade knew all about dog foxes that take hounds on their own trail to keep them away

from vixens or young. He guessed shrewdly that by
some mischance the hounds had swung away on
Star's trail.

Taking the dogs back to the hollow stump, where
he knew the cubs had been, Dade tried to pick up
the trail from there. But the hounds were made
uncertain by the change. They had been pulled
from a scent that they knew was fresh, brought back
to the same fox's cold spoor, and that bewildered
them. They wouldn't take the trail, and Dade had to
admit defeat once more. With the dogs still on
leash, he returned to his cabin.

Star remained near Dade's clearing until night
shadows shrouded the hills in protecting darkness,
then took off for Vixen and the cubs. They were
safe. In the darkness Star sniffed noses with his
mate, and lay down for a few minutes' rest. The
biggest cub, the one with the extra toe, crawled
over to his father and began playing with Star's
bushy tail. He bit suddenly, closing baby teeth over
the tail and pinching hard. In irritation Star rose,
walked a few feet, sat down again, and glared at his
son.

But he could not rest for long. The overhanging
bulge of the fallen tree was no place for either Vixen
or the cubs. Again Star grasped a wriggling cub in
his jaws, and followed by Vixen, trotted down the
slope.

Star entered and waded up a free-flowing little

stream, then climbed out on the same side he had entered. A hundred yards up, he went back into the stream. This time he emerged on the opposite side, leaped the stream, and entered a grove of small hemlocks. In the center of the grove was a giant oak that had escaped the lumberman's axe because it was hollow, and in the hollow Star left his cub. An hour later all the cubs were moved.

Star went forth to hunt, and luck was with him. He caught a cottontail, took it back to Vixen, returned to the same place, and caught one for himself. Hungrily he stretched out to eat the first food he had had in twenty-four hours. Then, remembering the snowshoe he had dropped when he discovered Dade Matson, he got it for Vixen.

Until the early morning hours, Star stayed near the hollow oak, but he was restless and uncertain. He had been hunted before, but never so relentlessly or so tirelessly. Dade Matson was making him nervous.

Two days later, an hour before daylight, Star went out on another hunting trip. He crossed Dade's fresh trail leading into the hills, and hurried anxiously back to Vixen. Nothing had been near the den and his mate and cubs were undisturbed. Star resumed the hunt.

He entered a thicket in which he had usually been able to find rabbits, but turned tail and fled almost at once. Both paws fast in a fox trap's steel jaws, a big snowshoe sat staring at him with terrified eyes. Star ran only a few yards before he recovered from his panic and turned to investigate.

The trap had been on no trail, but in a thicket where a hunting fox might venture. Star made a wide circle to pick up Dade's scent near the trap. He followed, very suspicious of any gaps in the trail. Only when he had assured himself positively that Dade hadn't been near the place, did he venture to hunt in another thicket. Even then he was nervous and afraid.

Out to catch him at any cost and any way he could, Dade Matson was blanketing Star's home range with traps and snares. Going out to hunt again, Star found a spotted fawn tangled in a wire snare. The anxious mother of the dead fawn snorted near it, and charged Star when he came.

Star fled ignominiously. He had borne all he could and could take no more. The good hunting grounds that he had staked out for himself and Vixen, the place where he had chosen to raise his family, had had only normal dangers. Now it was a place of deadly terror. The next time Star went out to hunt, he went in the opposite direction.

He was trespassing and he knew it, and he must fight if he were detected. This range belonged to Patches, an old dog fox that had already sired half a dozen broods of cubs in it and was now busy feeding another litter. But Star did not hesitate once he decided to cross into Patches' country. He traveled swiftly, hoping to make a kill and be out again before Patches discovered him. Star planned a big circle that would bring him back to the hollow oak where Vixen lay with the cubs.

He was in luck, for he caught a half-grown wild turkey that had roosted too low. Stretching beside the small gobbler, Star plucked a portion, ate, and carried what was left to Vixen. While the cubs tumbled beside her and nibbled experimentally on feathers, Star kept a watchful eye on his back trail.

The next night, when Star started again on the endless search for food, he came face to face with Patches.

About as big as Star, but much older, he was still in the prime of life. Beneath his silky fur, his tough skin was seamed with battle scars, and long ago he had lost his right ear in some desperate encounter. Patches was an experienced and tough veteran of the woods.

He flung himself forward, and his slicing teeth found and scored Star's shoulder. Star succeeded only in sinking his teeth through what remained of Patches' right ear. Then Patches dived for the flank, and Star whirled wildly to get out of the way. A flank attack was his own favorite way of fighting. He knew what he had done to Stub and what it might do to him.

Rearing, they flailed each other's faces with front

paws until Star felt his right paw slide into the cutting machine that was Patches' mouth. Lashing desperately out with his jaws, he cut Patches' cheek. When the other released his paw, Star whirled and ran.

Had Patches come into his range, Star would have fought to the end. But it was he, and not Patches, who had invited the fight. He was guilty and he knew it, and that robbed him of his courage. Star ran for the same reason that a big dog will run from a little one that is guarding its own back yard.

For a little way Patches pursued him, nipping at his flanks. At the ridge that marked the dividing line between their hunting grounds, Patches stopped. Star raced on until he was positive that there was no longer any pursuit. Then, reluctantly, he went to some of his own familiar hunting grounds.

He found a snowshoe hare and a turkey gobbler, both dead in Dade Matson's snares. Star prowled fearfully along, never knowing when a strangling snare would catch him, too. But he had to find food. All night he hunted, and dawn was breaking in the sky when he finally caught a rabbit for Vixen. When he carried it to her, she did not eat at once. While the cubs squirmed restlessly, and waited for her to come back, she gently licked the cuts and slashes that Patches had inflicted on her mate. Only then was she satisfied to eat.

The next time Star went hunting, he did not go

into the woods at all. His own range, where he had been able to hunt as he wished and go where he wished, was far too dangerous. If he ventured onto another dog fox's hunting grounds, he would have to fight for whatever he got. Star knew a surer way to get food for his family.

Keeping off trails, where steel traps might be concealed, and out of thickets, where strangling snares lay in wait, he raced straight down the hill, toward the valley. Coming to a fresh trail laid by Dade Matson, Star leaped clear over it, and was soon on the outer border of the Crowley fields.

There was no light in the house, and everything was quiet. Making sure that Thunder wasn't prowling around the yard, Star turned his attention to the barnyard. The horses were stabled, the cows, turned out to pasture after milking, were lying down and chewing their cuds. From the poultry house and sheds there drifted a mouth-watering scent of chickens, turkeys, geese and ducks.

Making not even a whisper of noise, keeping the wind in his nose, Star padded across the meadow and went to the same shed from which he had taken the hen on that first night of the big storm, so long ago. Again chickens were there, asleep on such makeshift roosts as they could find. Star was only a moving shadow as he entered the shed and took his victim.

The first time he had been a rank amateur, a

bungling youngster who had only a vague idea of
what he was doing. Now he was an expert, a highly
skilled and cunning hunter. He knew exactly where
to bite and how hard. The chicken died without a
flutter. Another one clucked querulously in the
night, but Star was gone. He slipped from the shed
as softly as he had entered, and instead of cutting
back toward the den he ran deliberately away from
it. Star circled to the creek, waded it for fifty yards,
then leaped out and raced up a hill. He waded
another creek, stopped for ten minutes to see if any
hound was on his track, then took the chicken to his
family.

The next night he went clear to the head of the
valley and caught one of Eli Catman's big rabbits,
and the night after that he visited the Masons' poultry yard. The following hunt took him to Mike Tallant's. He never went to the same place twice in
succession, and he always hid his trail when returning to the den.

So far he had not been discovered. The valley was
usually a place of plenty, and this year there was a
vast abundance. One or two chickens, ducks, or
rabbits, were hard to miss.

With all they could possibly eat, the cubs grew
like weeds in the sun. They wrestled and scrambled
like so many playful puppies. They sprang at but-
terflies, and with noses to the earth followed
ground-crawling bugs. They tried to climb trees;

and, whenever they could, they tormented Star. Piling all over him whenever he lay down near them, they chewed his ears, his tail, his paws, and everything else they could reach. All he could do was get up and move farther away. Never did he snap back, or offer to hurt one of the youngsters.

Their play was a necessary thing. As they rolled and tumbled about they also developed young bodies and muscles. They had to be strong if they were to survive. In the wilderness, weaklings do not live very long.

Though she was a good mother, Vixen was a severe one. When the cubs frolicked, she was always near, watching them. Whenever any one of them, particularly Star's tiny counterpart, ventured farther than Vixen thought it should, she called it back. If the cub did not come at once, it was sure to know Vixen's punishing teeth.

Vixen, however, let the cubs play with and tug at her as much as they wished. Though their teeth were sharp enough to hurt and their jaws strong enough to sink their teeth deeply, she bore it where Star would not.

The cubs were very active when, again at the Crowley farm, Star caught a live chicken. Usually he killed instantly and silently, but this chicken he clamped just hard enough to hold it. The terrified broiler wakened the night with protesting squawks. Alarmed, the rest of the chickens set up a discordant racket that brought Jack and Jeff on the run. Thunder, who had dug holes in the vegetable garden, and was being punished by having to stay on the end of a long chain, could not join them.

In the black night, Jack and Jeff could determine only that there had been a raid on their poultry. However, the next morning they made a more thorough investigation and found Star's distinctive tracks. After that they took better care of their poultry and spread the word that the Haunt Fox was raiding again.

Careful, as usual, to conceal his tracks, Star took the live chicken to his den. When the cubs scrambled out to see what he had brought, Star let the chicken go.

The fascinated cubs gathered around, unable for the moment to fathom this mystery. They stretched curious noses toward the chicken, and when one touched it with a cold nose the chicken fluttered its wings. At once all five cubs scurried away, but not for long. Circling the chicken again, they slapped it with their paws and nosed it. The little cub that looked like Star grasped a wing tip firmly between his teeth. The chicken struggled to get away, and dragged the cub with it. But the cub held on, and the others got the idea. All five swarmed upon the chicken and pulled it down. It was the only way they could learn what they must know.

A couple of nights later Star visited Eli Catman's.

But the valley was alert now. Farmers were watching their stock more carefully, and most had discovered for themselves that some was missing. Eli was ready, and when Star fled with the rabbit, Eli's hound was hot on his trail.

Star tried his usual tricks. But he knew the hound behind him, and he was well aware that no ordinary ruse would throw him off. However, Star had picked up some new tricks, and was keeping one in reserve for just such an occasion. Near the top of a hill was a rock ledge about thirty feet high. On its face were three places where a leaping fox might land, and Star had already determined, by jumping down the ledge, that he could do it. He was fairly certain that no big and heavy hound could follow him.

Star jumped from the top, catching and balancing himself on an outjutting rock that was scarcely wide enough to hold his four bunched feet. He bounced to the next landing place, and the next, and flashed away from the foot of the ledge. On top Eli's hound cast helplessly about.

The season wore on and the cubs grew, and as they grew they learned. They now knew how to catch mice by pinning them between clumps of grass. They understood grouse, and the best ways to take them, although they were not yet very successful. Each cub had caught at least one rabbit, and had scored many near misses. They were learning fast.

Chapter 12   The Hunt

The frost-seared earth bore a light dusting of snow that had fallen during the night, and a churning mass of black clouds in the sky promised more snow to come. Leafless hardwoods rattled cold twigs in the stiff north wind, and evergreens swayed somberly against the hills. In the Crowley field, corn shocks were arranged in orderly procession, their withered leaves powdered with snow. A flock of vari-colored pigeons wheeled in erratic flight over them. In the farmyard, Jack Crowley broke shell ice that had formed on the watering trough as he led the horses out to drink.

It had been a good season in the valley. Barns

were filled to bursting with hay and grain. Every fruit and vegetable bin was overflowing, and cellars groaned with shelf after shelf of canned goods prepared by thrifty farm wives. From the day the spring sun had made fields again tillable, every working member of every farm family had put in as many hours as possible and for most of them that meant dawn to dark labor. After school was out, the children were expected to contribute their full share, and there had been little time for anything except work.

Now, at last, the hot, hard summer was over and there would be more leisure. Jack's eyes glowed with anticipation as he glanced at the hills, for to him leisure meant hunting foxes with Thunder. He was no longer the youngster who had chosen an awkward foxhound puppy and so uncertainly brought it home with him. Jack had grown in every way, and in the boy he still was could be seen a strong promise of the man he would be.

The horses drank their fill, and voluntarily turned back toward the barn. Jeff, who had been cleaning stalls, leaned on his shovel as one of the big horses crowded past him. Jeff, too, was keen and eager, for this weather brought back to him some of the best parts of his own life.

"Aiming to get out in the hills with Thunder?" he asked.

Jack grinned. "I'd like to. Can you go too?"

"Not this weekend. Jack Mallory's coming in to see about buying some cows today or tomorrow. But you'd better go. School keeps all next week, remember."

"Well, maybe I will give it a whirl as soon as the chores are done."

Jeff sniffed. "Don't know how I ever managed the chores before you grew to working size. Take today and tomorrow off; you've been hitting it pretty hard and this is the first snow. Ask your mother to fix you a lunch and start now, else you won't have any time."

"Thanks! But I don't like to—"

"Go ahead," Jeff urged. "There's hardly enough work around here today to keep one man busy."

Jeff leaned his shovel against the wall and they both went to the barn door to look at the snow-powdered hills. The pigeons, that had alighted among the shocked corn, rose in formation and flew to another part of the field. They dropped to the snow and busied themselves picking up corn. Jack watched them idly.

"All right," he said. "I'll go see if Thunder and I can find a—Look!"

A red fox had leaped out of the corn shock where it had been waiting. It sprang on a pigeon, then streaked toward the hills.

"Look at that fellow go!" said Jeff, half in admiration and half in condemnation. "He must have been waiting in that corn shock since before daylight, cuss his red hide!"

Jack said eagerly, "Let's go see!"

They crossed the field at a dog trot while the pigeons, only momentarily disturbed at losing one of their number, alighted near another corn shock and resumed feeding. Side by side the Crowleys reached the place where the fox had hidden. A few blue feathers from the slain pigeon lay among the evenly spaced tracks of a running fox. Though some of the tracks were scuffed, there could be no doubt about who had made them.

"The Haunt Fox again!" Jeff said.

Jack's blood raced, remembering the thrilling sound of a hound tonguing on a fox's trail, and the many times he had drawn his shotgun down on a fox running ahead of Thunder. There had been all kinds, from blundering youngsters up to a wise old dog fox that had outsmarted them. But never the Haunt Fox. Though Jack had crossed Star's trail while hunting, it had always been a cold trail. Jack's eyes glowed.

"I've found my fox; the Haunt Fox!" he exulted.

"It'll be a hunt, Bub," Jeff warned.

"That's what I'm looking for!"

Jack raced toward the house. Thunder, sensing excitement in the offing, strained to the end of his chain to meet him. The big hound was lean and tough, in perfect condition for the first hunt of the season. Jack patted his head and went into the house.

He slipped a sheath knife onto his belt, donned a wool hunting jacket, and filled one pocket with shells. In another pocket he put a carton of water-proofed matches. Then, shotgun in hand, he bustled into the kitchen.

With both her men confirmed hunters, his mother understood his excitement. In no time she had sandwiches ready, and Jack smiled his thanks as he kissed her.

"You'll be wearing the Haunt Fox's pelt for a neckpiece," he promised. "On you it'll look good, too."

"Good luck," she said, "and be careful."

Seeing the gun, Thunder came clear to the end of his chain and reared to flail the air with thrashing paws. His excited baying roused echoes that rolled up the distant hills, and when Jack reached down to unsnap his chain, Thunder danced a crazy circle around him.

Jack glanced up to see Jeff, who had followed Star's track a little way up the hill. Thunder saw him, too, and bounded enthusiastically forward to meet him. The big hound scented the fox track and swung instantly to it. His head went down, his tail stiffened. For a moment or two he snuffled noisily about. Then a deep bay rolled from his chest and he raced away on the track.

Jack came up to Jeff, and the two turned to look at the running, baying hound. In this, the first few minutes of a hunt, Thunder was rested and fresh, and was traveling as fast as he could. He disappeared in the forest, and only his roaring bays floated back to tell the watchers where he was.

"I'm not coming back until I get him," Jack said confidently.

"That so?" his father smiled. "Well, watch yourself in the hills."

The cubs, as well equipped to take care of themselves as any young foxes ever are, had gone their own way. With their departure came a vast lessening of Star's responsibilities.

A capable huntress in her own right, Vixen could take care of herself. But unlike her mate, Vixen was a cautious creature who never placed herself in danger if there was any possible way to avoid it. She never left the wilderness, while Star raided farms whenever the impulse moved him.

Because the cubs were no longer dependent on him, it was not necessary to hunt in a restricted range. Nor, after making a raid, did Star have to run right back into the hills with whatever he caught. He had been lying up near the farmlands for the better part of two days now. Yesterday he had noticed the wheeling pigeons as he walked near the

Crowleys. Always, after a short flight, they came down to gather kernels of corn among the shocks.

Star's had been a simple plan to make and to execute. Before dawn, as Jeff had suspected, he had merely hidden himself in a corn shock. With daylight the pigeons came out to feed. Star had only to wait until they alighted near his ambush, then leap out and make his kill.

Safe in the brush, he stopped to pluck and eat the pigeon. Star licked his chops, and sneezed out a bit of feather that was tickling his nose. At a slow trot he headed deeper into the hills, intending to find Vixen. But he had scarcely started when Thunder's baying shattered the morning silence. Star stopped and looked back, his eyes sparkling with mischief.

From the day the cubs were born until they left to go their own way, life had been a deadly serious business. There had been no time for anything except taking care of his family and avoiding Dade Matson's traps and snares. Though Star had had dogs on his trail during the summer, he had been able to think only of getting rid of them as quickly as possible. Now there was time for fun, with no chance of leading a hound to helpless cubs. Star lined out to run, and streaked away.

He knew from the voice that the hound was Thunder, and he had a great respect for Thunder. But he did not feel any fear. Though he knew that it would be hard to shake this hound from his tracks, he had complete confidence in his ability to do it. The hound was not the real danger he must face. The hunter who would be with the hound was deadly and at all costs Star must avoid him.

In a sudden burst of speed he left Thunder behind, then settled down to an easier gait. He circled through the brush, and from a high point looked down on the Crowley farm. There was nothing to be seen except the buildings, and Star ran on.

He was fresh and wanted to run, and the pigeon hadn't been big enough to fill his belly and make him logy. For an hour he made no special effort to leave any breaks in his trail. Then he waded a creek, knowing as he did so that such a ruse would not delay Thunder very long.

Star left the water and wove an erratic trail through a laurel thicket. He twisted and turned, crossing and re-crossing his own path a dozen times, and raced out of the laurel just as Thunder entered it. Star ran to a little hillock and waited for Thunder to untangle the snarled trail he had left.

A mediocre hound would have been confused, but Thunder was not mediocre. He needed only minutes to discover what Star had done in the thicket, and what he must do about it. Instead of nosing about the twisted maze of tracks, he cut across and picked up the trail beyond the thicket.

Star had given a quarter of an hour to laying the trail, and Thunder worked it out in a third that much time.

Star got up to run again. This time he laid his course through a grove of second-growth hardwoods, traveling at a fast lope. Suddenly he called on every ounce of speed he could summon and flashed at right angles to the path he had intended to take.

Jack Crowley was standing in the hardwoods when Star came, and saw the fox as the fox saw him. Jack did not shoot because Star had not appeared where Jack thought he would, and was out of range. At a fast walk Jack started toward the next place where he assumed the Haunt Fox would appear.

Star ran straightaway, wanting to put as much distance as possible between himself and the hunter. Faint in the distance he heard Thunder's steady baying; though the hound was not nearly as fast as the fox, he had great endurance. Star waded another creek, knew from his tonguing that the broken trail delayed Thunder only slightly, and made his way toward a gully full of scattered boulders.

Before venturing among the boulders, where few trees and no brush grew and he might be seen from a long way off, Star reconnoitered from all sides. Finally satisfying himself that the boulders hid no hunter, he made a long spring to the top of one, leaped from that to another, and so to a third. Gauging his leaps according to the distance between the boulders, he jumped from one to the other, then ran into the woods.

For the first time, Thunder slowed. He knew most of a fox's tricks, but this was a new one and he needed a while to figure it out. For fifteen minutes his deep-toned baying sounded among the boulders, where he was casting for scent. The varied gaps in Star's trail he could not understand.

Meantime Star ran through a herd of deer browsing on a sheltered hillside, so that their scent mingled with his. Running up the hillside, Star sought a thicket and sat down with his tail curled around his rear paws.

Faintly in the distance he heard Thunder baying, and knew from the sound that he had not yet shaken the hound from his trail. Star danced nervously, and for the first time knew a little worry. The average hound would have been hopelessly lost long before this, but obviously Thunder was still coming. At a fast run, Star set off across the hilltop.

Morning waned into afternoon, early evening shadows gathered, and still Thunder came. Tiring, and hungry, Star needed time to rest and to hunt. But he dared not stop as long as Thunder pushed him so hard.

Star made a wide circle that took him back into the hills and toward the ledge where, during the summer, he had left Eli Catman's hound baffled. The ledge was a tricky place, and he was still sure that no hound could descend it. He leaped to the first paw hold, down to the second, and to the third. He sprang from the ledge—and landed squarely in one of Dade Matson's traps.

Twenty minutes later Thunder appeared on top of the ledge. Finding no way to get down, he wakened the wilderness with deep-toned baying.

When Jack Crowley started into the hills after the Haunt Fox, he was tense and excited. There was within him a strange sensation that he had known before, and always when he felt like that he had had good luck. He probably would be gone all day, and perhaps all night too and all tomorrow, but of one thing he was sure. When he came back, he would bring the Haunt Fox with him.

Jack followed the trail to the high point from which Star had looked down on the Crowley farm, and stood listening. Most foxes laid long trails, and almost always the hounds that chased them were out of the hunter's hearing part of the time. But they always circled back, and the hunter could plan his strategy by listening to his hound. At last, so far away that his roaring was borne only faintly on the wind, Jack heard Thunder working in the laurel where Star had left a maze of tracks. His voice faded out of hearing, then his tonguing was heard once more.

Jack raced over the hill's flat summit toward a stand of hardwoods, and stood quietly beside a tree. It was an orthodox move; a fox, running where Thunder's voice said it was, should come to the hardwoods. Thunder's baying strengthened, became louder, and Jack tensed himself. He had guessed correctly; the Haunt Fox was coming. A moment later Jack saw him and brought the shotgun to his shoulder.

Then he lowered it again; the fox was not only out of range, but had darted away at right angles. Still, Jack had guessed almost right; twenty-five yards closer to the place where Star came through and the hunt would have been over. But those twenty-five yards were too many; he simply hadn't been close enough.

Jack watched Thunder sweep through on the Haunt Fox's trail, then he made his way to a high knob from which he could overlook the surrounding country. For five minutes he heard Thunder bay, then the tonguing faded out of hearing again. The fox was evidently making long swings into the valleys and over the hills.

Jack chose another stand, while the cold wind cut at his face and reddened his hands. He cradled the shotgun in the crook of his arm and walked rapidly along to warm himself. He grinned in the face of the chilly wind, for he still felt a warm excitement that spoke of good fortune. The Haunt Fox was worthy of his name; he was as elusive as a ghost. But Jack still felt confident. If necessary he would make a rough camp tonight and, though he might be hungry, he had enough sandwiches to see him through. Jeff had said that it would be a hunt, and a hunt it was turning out to be. But it would be a memorable hunt no matter what happened. It was already that.

Thunder was out of hearing now, and Jack climbed another high knob from which he could get a good view of the surrounding hills. He made his way toward the last place he had heard Thunder, and drew his jacket about him as the wind freshened and became colder. Night was coming, and more snow would come with it, but Jack did not care.

He halted, trying to catch and pin down a sound so elusive that he could not be sure whether it was Thunder tonguing or merely some trick of the wind. He heard it again, and definitely identified it as the baying of a hound. The volume increased as Thunder came nearer, so Jack stayed where he was. The hound was running on an adjoining ridge, and there still might be a chance to outwit the Haunt Fox tonight.

Thunder's baying was coming steadily from one place now. Listening, Jack tried to interpret what

was happening. Slowly his heart sank. The Haunt
Fox, after all, was not the magnificent creature he
had thought. It was not a superior fox at all, but had
gone to earth, sought refuge in a burrow, like any
frightened cub.

Jack made his way toward the sound of Thunder's
voice. He saw the hound while he was still a hundred yards away, looking from the top of a rock
ledge and still baying. Jack walked up beside the
dog and looked down.

The fox was lying perfectly still, pressed close to
the earth he loved and not moving at all. Jack
peered down through the lengthening shadows and
saw the trap on Star's foot. For a long moment he
just stood there, his hand on Thunder's neck. Then
he snapped the chain on Thunder's collar and led
him around the ledge. Tying the hound to a small
tree, he walked slowly up to the Haunt Fox.

When he was three feet away, Star leaped to the
end of the trap chain and his slicing fangs left a clean
rip in Jack's heavy pants. Then Jack's foot was on
him. With his boot, Jack pressed the fox to earth. As
gently as possible he held him there, while his
hands slipped around the Haunt Fox's neck. With
his knee he depressed the trap's springs, and as soon
as the jaws loosened he lifted Star out. Almost in the
same motion he cast the fox away from him.

For a second they faced each other, the courageous hunted and the sporting hunter. Then the Haunt Fox slipped like a shadow into the gathering gloom and was gone.

It was pitch dark when Jack and Thunder got back to the Crowley farm. Jack made his hound comfortable on the back porch and went wearily into the house. Jeff looked up from the magazine he was reading.

"Well, Bub?"

"I saw him."

"Close?"

Then, while his mother was fixing him a hot supper, Jack told them the whole story. "That's all," he said finally, "except that I guess I owe Dade Matson four dollars bounty money, plus whatever a good fox pelt brings."

For a moment Jeff said nothing, but his eyes spoke volumes. Then he pointed to the slash in Jack's pants.

"Here's a job for you, Mother," he said. "Meantime, Son, you'll find a good pair of hunting britches in my closet. I think they'll fit now."

About the Author

JIM KJELGAARD's first book was *Forest Patrol* (1941), based on the wilderness experiences of himself and his brother, a forest ranger. Since then he has written many others—all of them concerned with the out-of-doors. *Big Red, Irish Red,* and *Outlaw Red* are dog stories about Irish setters. *Kalak of the Ice* (a polar bear) and *Chip, the Dam Builder* (a beaver) are wild-animal stories. *Snow Dog* and *Wild Trek* describe the adventures of a trapper and his half-wild dog. *Haunt Fox* is the story both of a fox and of the dog and boy who trailed him, and *Stormy* is concerned with a wildfowl retriever and his young owner. *Fire-Hunter* is a story about prehistoric man; *Boomerang Hunter* about the equally primitive Australian aborigine. *Rebel Siege* and *Buckskin Brigade* are tales of American frontiersmen, and *Wolf Brother* presents the Indian side of "the winning of the West." The cougar-hunting *Lion Hound* and the greyhound story, *Desert Dog,* are laid in the present-day Southwest. *A Nose for Trouble* and *Trailing Trouble* are adventure mysteries centered around a game warden and his man-hunting bloodhound. The same game warden also appears in *Wildlife Cameraman* and *Hidden Trail,* stories about a young nature photographer and his dog.

JIM KJELGAARD

In these adventure stories, Jim Kjelgaard shows us the special world of animals, the wilderness, and the bonds between men and dogs. *Irish Red* and *Outlaw Red* are stories about two champion Irish setters. *Snow Dog* shows what happens when a half-wild dog crosses paths with a trapper. The cougar-hunting *Lion Hound* and the greyhound story *Desert Dog* take place in our present-day Southwest. And, *Stormy* is an extraordinary story of a boy and his devoted dog. You'll want to read all these exciting books.

☐	15332	A NOSE FOR TROUBLE	$2.25
☐	15121	HAUNT FOX	$1.95
☐	15194	BIG RED	$2.50
☐	15324	DESERT DOG	$2.50
☐	15286	IRISH RED: SON OF BIG RED	$2.50
☐	15247	LION HOUND	$2.50
☐	15339	OUTLAW RED	$2.50
☐	15230	SNOW DOG	$2.25
☐	15215	STORMY	$2.25
☐	15316	WILD TREK	$2.50

Prices and availability subject to change without notice.
Buy them at your local bookstore or use this handy coupon for ordering:

Bantam Books, Inc., Dept. KJ, 414 East Golf Road, Des Plaines, Ill. 60016
Please send me the books I have checked above. I am enclosing $_____
(please add $1.25 to cover postage and handling). Send check or money order
—no cash or C.O.D.'s please.

Mr/Mrs/Miss_____

Address_____

City_____ State/Zip_____

KJ—8/85
Please allow four to six weeks for delivery. This offer expires 12/85.

Bantam Skylark Paperbacks
The Kid-Pleasers

Especially designed for easy reading with large type, wide margins and captivating illustrations, Skylarks are "kid-pleasing" paperbacks featuring the authors, subjects and characters children love.

☐	15258	**BANANA BLITZ** Florence Parry Heide	**$2.25**
☐	15259	**FREAKY FILLINS #1** David Hartley	**$1.95**
☐	15250	**THE GOOD-GUY CAKE** Barbara Dillion	**$1.95**
☐	15239	**C.L.U.T.Z.** Marilyn Wilkes	**$1.95**
☐	15237	**MUSTARD** Charlotte Graeber	**$1.95**
☐	15157	**ALVIN FERNALD: TV ANCHORMAN** Clifford Hicks	**$1.95**
☐	15338	**ANASTASIA KRUPNIK** Lois Lowry	**$2.50**
☐	15168	**HUGH PINE** Janwillen Van de Wetering	**$1.95**
☐	15188	**DON'T BE MAD IVY** Christine McDonnell	**$1.95**
☐	15248	**CHARLIE AND THE CHOCOLATE FACTORY** Roald Dahl	**$2.50**
☐	15174	**CHARLIE AND THE GREAT GLASS ELEVATOR** Roald Dahl	**$2.50**
☐	15317	**JAMES AND THE GIANT PEACH** Roald Dahl	**$2.95**
☐	15255	**ABEL'S ISLAND** William Steig	**$2.25**
☐	15194	**BIG RED** Jim Kjelgaard	**$2.50**
☐	15206	**IRISH RED: SON OF BIG RED** Jim Kjelgaard	**$2.25**
☐	01803	**JACOB TWO-TWO MEETS THE HOODED FANG** Mordecai Richler	**$2.95**
☐	15034	**TUCK EVERLASTING** Natalie Babbitt	**$2.25**
☐	15343	**THE TWITS** Roald Dahl	**$2.50**

Prices and availability subject to change without notice.

Buy them at your local bookstore or use this handy coupon for ordering: